ALIENS IN THE BACKYARD

UFO ENCOUNTERS, ABDUCTIONS, & SYNCHRONICITY

BY

TRISH MacGREGOR
& ROB MacGREGOR

Crossroad Press

OTHER BOOKS BY TRISH MAC-GREGOR

That was when he noticed beams of light, very low in intensity, in the expansive field behind the house. He opened the patio door, but the dog refused to go out. Charles grabbed him, forced him out, and shut the door. As Spot passed the motion detector sensor, the patio spotlights came on, illuminating the backyard. Charles couldn't see the beams any longer so he hit the switch, turning off the lights. After a few seconds, his eyes adjusted and he saw the beams of light again.

Now they burned with greater intensity and seemed to be moving closer and closer to his backyard. He counted nine distinct beams shaped like inverted ice cream cones, displayed asymmetrically across the field. They looked brighter near the ground and lost intensity toward the top. Some glowed more powerfully than others. He couldn't see anything above the cones except darkness. He didn't have any idea what he was looking at.

At first, he thought these cones might be solid acrylic tubes that were illuminated. He could even see movement inside the beams, like heat waves rising off a road surface on a scorching summer day. Whatever they were, Charles thought they were beautiful and was paralyzed by the spectacle. He watched for a couple minutes, then retreated and called out to Helene. "Are you awake?"

She mumbled that she was.

"I want you to see something. I want to know if you see the same thing that I do."

OTHER BOOKS BY ROB MAC-GREGOR

YOUNG ADULT NOVELS
Double Heart
Hawk Moon
Prophecy Rock

ADULT NOVELS
Time Catcher
Romancing the Raven
Crystal Skull
Indiana Jones and the Last Crusade
–The Peril at Delphi
–Dance of the Giants
–The Seven Veils
–The Genesis Deluge
–The Unicorn's Legacy
–The Interior World
Peter Benchley's Amazon: Ghost
JUST/IN TIME with Billy Dee Williams
PSI/NET with Billy Dee Williams

For Megan, with love always

TABLE OF CONTENTS

Chapter 5: The Fog
—AUTEC and UFO Hunters
—Encounters from the Depths
—Into the Triangle
—In-Flight Abduction
—The Tunnel Vortex
—Time Warp
—The Big Picture
—Target of Opportunity

Chapter 6: High Strangeness
—Strangers Who Know Too Much
—About Spot
—Another Strange Encounter
—Holy Water
—More Synchronicity
—When Negative is Positive
—Into the Vial

Chapter 7: Fostering Hybrids
—Missing Pregnancy
—The Breeding Program
—Alien Hybrid Nurseries
—Harvesting of Souls
—Hybrids Among Us

Chapter 8: What's Coming
—Presidents and UFOs
—Strategy
—What Does the Government Know?
—Government Spying
—Dreams of Disclosure

Chapter 9: Earth Shakings
—Warnings
—Native American Prophecies
—Abductees as Planetary Empaths
—Encounters and Planetary Empaths
—Earth Changes
—Unusual Symptoms and Sightings

Chapter 10: Identifying Flying Objects
—Mass Sightings
—Up Close and Personal
—Inside the Craft

Chapter 11: Skeptics and Disbelievers
—An Astonishing Survey
—What Scientists Say
—Hypnotic Regressions
—The Science Dilemma

Chapter 12: What's Up?
—The Enigma
—Where Are They From?
—A Personal Story
—Aliens and the Afterlife
—Who Are They, What Do They Want?
—The 3 Curious Aliens
—Seeking Consensus
—What Does It Mean?

INTRODUCTION

In speculative fiction, the darkness you think about in the privacy of your soul, the thing that terrifies you the most, the shadows that haunt you at four in the morning, the details you know are totally impossible, suddenly happen. You're Will Smith in *Independence Day*, watching in horror as the giant shadows of alien spacecraft fall across your planet. Or you're Dakota Fanning in Steven Spielberg's mini-series, *Taken*, a young girl lifted up into a beam of light, abducted by Grays. Or you're Fox Mulder, who knows the truth is out there because he witnessed the alien abduction of his own sister.

Whether we believe it or not, like it or not, the world of science fiction and fantasy creeps steadily into our daily world. It has caught the attention of mainstream science. Academics are asking what makes people believe in things that have not been proven, that don't exist. Meanwhile, possibly millions of individuals carry secrets that most are too terrified to reveal. But if they could articulate those secrets in a collective voice, it's likely they would tell us that aliens are here and that by and large, they are *not* our friends. They aren't *E.T.*

Without a doubt, aliens are embedded in our cultural landscape. You might see a poster on the side of a bus, featuring a Gray with its bulbous head, large black, wraparound eyes and barely noticeable nose and mouth. It's probably an ad for a new television show or movie. When the History Channel cancelled *UFO Hunters* after three seasons, thousands signed a petition to bring it back. Instead, it was replaced by *Ancient Aliens*, another documentary, one that fuses archaeology with alien contact and does so in a spectacular fashion. Movies about alien encounters and TV shows like Spielberg's *Taken* or *The X-Files, The 4400, and V,* have proliferated in the last twenty years. In 2013, more blockbuster UFO/alien movies are scheduled to be released—and one of the most highly anticipated movies is *Enders' Game,* based on Orson Scott Card's novel and starring Harrison Ford.

T. J. MACGREGOR & ROB MACGREGOR

So it's not surprising that polls indicate that more than 90 percent of Americans believe that intelligent life exists outside of our world. An MSNBC poll conducted in 2007, asked: *Do you believe that UFO sightings are actually visits from extraterrestrials?* 63 percent of the respondents said yes.

The alien abduction phenomenon has burgeoned into a sub-culture with its own set of beliefs, a separate reality that suggests we are no longer—and maybe never were—the most advanced species existing on planet Earth. A Roper Organization survey in 2003 found that more than 33 million Americans fit the profile of abductees. Exactly *what* these individuals are experiencing, though, is subject to intense debate.

Mainstream scientists reject the idea that the abductions are a physical reality and suggest psychological explanations: hypnogogic dream states, buried memories of childhood abuse, lucid dreaming, events imagined under hypnosis, mass hysteria stimulated by media reports, movies and television shows. Some also suggest these experiences are the result of psychiatric dysfunctions—psychosis, multiple personality disorder, and a variety of other exotic brain disorders. Yet, multiple studies indicate that abductees are no more likely than anyone else to suffer from psychiatric disorders.

Still, it seems that an insurmountable gap exists between what the abductees believe is real and what scientists believe. Abductees—or experiencers, as they often refer to themselves—are convinced they were taken by aliens and were subjected to tests and operations, often aboard a spacecraft. Mainstream scientists contend there is no evidence of intelligent beings existing elsewhere in the universe, much less existing so close to Earth that such beings are abducting people on a regular basis. They don't accept anecdotal evidence or even video evidence, for that matter, no matter how compelling. You can't always believe what you see.

No doubt about it, claims that aliens are abducting humans sound over-the-top. Yet, more and more people are coming forward with their stories, some are willing to use their names, and tell us that the absurd, the unreal, is quite real. As the narrator on *Ancient Aliens* is fond of saying: *What if they are right?*

After all, the history of science says that science is constantly evolving, altering our concept of what is real and possible as new evidence emerges. That's the scientific process. For instance, it wasn't until 200 years ago that science officially accepted the seemingly irrational folk stories, told for centuries, about stones falling from the sky. Well, yes, they do. We call them meteorites and have no doubt about their existence.

Prior to that shift in thinking, stones that fell from the sky were usually explained as volcanic rocks violently spewed out during major eruptions or terrestrial rocks that had been struck by lightning. That's why they were called "thunderstones." Scientists didn't even consider the idea that rocks fell to Earth from outer space; the notion didn't fit into consensus reality.

With all that in mind, here are some of the abductees and experiencers you will meet.

Connie J Cannon is a retired nurse from St. Augustine, Florida. For years, she was so terrified of ridicule that she kept her experiences to herself and struggled to understand the complexities of what had happened to her. First abducted at the age of four, she is now seventy, is tired of hiding her experiences, and is willing to use her real name. She "came out" in 2010, with a moving and dramatic story about an abduction that happened in 1981 to her and her 12-year-old son, John, when they suddenly found themselves on a military base. We posted *The Abduction* on our synchronicity blog and it received more than a hundred comments, some of them from other abductees.

Her story is complemented by accounts from several other abductees, who hid this part of their lives for years and are now stepping forward to reveal what happened to them. They talk about their encounters, especially with the now familiar Grays, and without exception, consider their experiences negative. However, some also maintain they have encountered benevolent beings as well, and that the issue of who they are and the nature of their intentions is complex.

In addition to Connie, you'll meet:

–Charles and Helene Fontaine (pseudonyms), a Canadian couple in their forties, who didn't even believe in UFOs before their encounter in March 2011.

–Diane Fine (pseudonym) was first taken when she was a toddler and is now in her early fifties. She has worked as a paranormal researcher, corporate bookkeeper, and bookstore manager.

–Bruce Gernon, now in his sixties, is a real estate broker and private pilot whose experience while flying from West Palm Beach to Andros Island in the Bahamas was the subject of a book, *The Fog*, co-authored by Rob MacGregor.

The thread that ties all these people together is the way their experiences have sculpted and dominated their lives. Connie's intense need to understand her abductions has taken her into studies of ancient cultures

XVI   T. J. MACGREGOR & ROB MACGREGOR

and languages, mathematics, and into the area of death and dying as a hospice nurse. For a time when she was in her twenties, she worked as a pilot and an assistant to a famous NASA-affiliated astrophysicist. She recalls her experiences spontaneously and has never recovered abduction memories through hypnosis. She now has Parkinson's and suspects it's related to alien implants in her sinuses and behind her ear. She says X-rays have documented the implants.

The lives of Charles and Helene Fontaine, conservative French Canadian Catholics, have been irrevocably changed by their experience. Charles has struggled with serious bouts of depression. His worldview has been shattered and he and his wife live in fear of being identified as UFO nuts in their community and where they work. For more than a year after their encounter, Charles remained so terrified of another encounter that he, his wife and daughter all carried vials of holy water for protection.

Diane Fine's search for answers launched her on a spiritual voyage, specifically into the Nyingama branch of Tibetan Buddhism. She studied under Lama Chodak Gyatso Nupa, who from 1979 to 1990 worked closely with the Dalai Lama. From him, she learned certain meditation and breathing techniques that help ameliorate her terror during and after abductions. Her experiences, like Connie's, enhanced her intuitive and psychic ability. As a paranormal researcher, Diane has worked with Dr. Stephen Greer, Colin Andrews, and Dr. James Harder of University of California at Berkeley. Diane, like Connie, has some serious health issues that may be related to her abductions.

Bruce Gernon's experience in the Bermuda Triangle happened in 1970, when he was 24 years old and scouting for real estate in the Bahamas with his dad, a real estate developer. In the forty-two years since, his peculiar encounter has dominated his life. His search for answers has prompted him to investigate several theories about the lenticular-shaped cloud that surrounded his Bonanza A36, caused all the plane's electronic instruments to malfunction, and somehow created a time and space distortion that enabled him to arrive at his destination far too early.

There's no question that *something* has happened to these individuals. Scientists can offer us possible explanations unrelated to aliens, but there are no definitive answers. Many abductees are traumatized by missing memories, inexplicable physical markings and bruises on their bodies, and the sense that something terrifying has happened to them. Many suffer from nightmares, phobias, and depression and most of them are so afraid of being ridiculed, that they don't even confide in their families and friends.

THE CREEPING REALITY

If the abductees could speak as a collective voice, they might point out that an alien intelligence known as the Grays collect sperm and ova and DNA from abductees and are using this material to create a hybrid race. These Grays wipe away the memories of abductees and implant screen memories. They also implant devices in their abductees—in the ears, brains, sinuses and elsewhere, and track them like branded sheep. There are shape shifters among them.

Perhaps they are us from the future. Perhaps they are, as famous abductee Betty Hill believed, from Zeta Reticulli. Maybe they are from the land of the dead, mythical, archetypal, inter-dimensional travelers. And maybe we're all living in *The Matrix* and just don't know it yet.

When we laugh at alien abductees and their stories, and many of us do, they become even more hesitant to tell us their experiences. So when we meet a few who are willing to talk, to go on the record, we should listen to their stories, even if they sound like science fiction.

SOMETHING ABOUT US

On a shelf in our library is one of the classic books in UFO literature, published in 1968: John G. Fuller's *The Interrupted Journey: Two Lost Hours 'Aboard a Flying Saucer.'* Beneath the title is a short description: The strangest story of our time—the abduction of an American couple aboard a UFO—as revealed by them under hypnosis. The couple was Betty and Barney Hill and their story is often cited as the first abduction in modern times. Inside the book is an inscription:

> To Rob and Trish
> Keep your eyes on the skies.
> Warm Regards,
>
> Betty Hill

Betty Hill signed the book for us when we covered a UFO conference in Hollywood, Florida for OMNI Magazine in 1986, twenty-five years after her and Barney's experience. Betty and author Budd Hopkins, both of whom we got to know, were the featured speakers. We had read Fuller's book, but weren't entirely convinced of the Hills' story—that she and Barney had been taken aboard a UFO on September 19, 1961, and were subjected to terrifying physical examinations by aliens. Yet, it seemed that something had happened to them. But what?

For our part, we have never experienced an alien abduction. We approach the subject not as experiencers or as scholarly academic researchers, but from a journalistic perspective. We've been interested in the subject for decades, and in fact wrote about UFOs and paranormal phenomena for the Anti-Matter section of OMNI for several years in the late 1980s.

By the time the edgy science magazine shut its doors, we had moved on to writing books and novels. Through the years, some of the people who passed in and out of our lives claimed to be abductees. A few had uncovered their traumatic memories through hypnosis, others had remembered their experiences through dreams or spontaneous recall and chose not to explore them. Regardless of which path these abductees took, their lives in the aftermath of their encounters had been profoundly and permanently changed.

In 2009, we started a blog on synchronicity—meaningful coincidence—mostly as a research experiment. Two books grew out of the blog that were published in 2010 and 2011: *The 7 Secrets of Synchronicity* and *Synchronicity and the Other Side*. Because synchronicity is often a component in UFO encounters, the blog has featured a number of UFO and abduction stories. Those stories attracted the attention of other abductees, who have come forward with their experiences.

But long before our blog and even before our work with OMNI, we explored the roots of the modern abduction phenomenon when we journeyed to the island of Chiloe in southern Chile. Here, we researched the legend that men in black on a brightly lit ghost ship were abducting islanders. That's where our interest deepened.

CHAPTER 1
ABOARD THE *CALEUCHE*

We arrived in Santiago, Chile on July 23, 1983, in the midst of winter. A wet chill seeped through our clothing and into our bones. We were a couple of South Floridians, who hadn't packed enough warm clothing.

We'd been married a week and were on our honeymoon. We had chosen Chile as our starting point because Ladeco Airline, which had just started flying between Miami and Santiago, was offering an unbeatable introductory round trip fare of $299, for a flight of more than four thousand miles to the tip of South America. This was in the day before Internet and Google, so our travel information about the country was mostly limited to our Fodor guide and focused primarily on Santiago and the tourist spots along the Pacific coast. We had no particular plans other than to allow synchronicity to determine the course of our trip.

On the long flight from Miami to Santiago, with more than two hundred passengers aboard, we happened to sit next to a Chilean woman who inadvertently proved pivotal to our journey. We asked her if she could suggest any mysterious places in Chile where we might encounter something mystical or mythical.

"Oh, Chiloe," she said without hesitation.

We'd never heard of it. "Where is it?"

"It's an island off Puerto Montt, where land transportation ends in my country. From Puerto Montt, you take a ferry to Chiloe. The name means land of sea gulls. There, they believe in *pincoyas*—mermaids—and in a ghost ship, the *Caleuche,* that is manned by sorcerers or *brujos*, who are immortal and possess the power to alter their shapes at will. Supposedly, they can transform themselves into wolves, fish, rocks and birds, and when they take human form they are usually tall, foreign, blond. Sometimes they abduct the islanders."

"Do these abductions actually happen?" Trish asked.

"That depends on who you talk to."

She went on to say that some islanders believed that the ship itself could transform its shape. In fact, the name, *Caleuche*, comes from Mapudungun, a Native American language. *Caleutum* means to transform or change states, and *che* means people or person. We were struck by the cultural parallel to the alien abduction scenario, recognized the synchronicity, and knew that Chiloe was now our destination.

We spent two days in Santiago, then boarded an overnight train to Puerto Montt. That evening in the dining car, synchronicity was at work again. We were seated with a young Chilean couple on their way to Puerto Montt to visit relatives. They were curious about why we Americans were headed to a place as remote as Puerto Montt, especially in the dead of winter. "If you want to ski, you should be going into the mountains," the woman said.

"We're actually headed to Chiloe," Rob explained. "To research the legend of the Caleuche."

Her husband laughed. "Ghost ships, mermaids, abductions… it's all just silly stories."

"No, it's not." The woman sat forward, her eyes lit up. "My *abuelita* lived for years on Chiloe. She said the stories are all true."

"But your grandmother wasn't right in the head toward the end of her life," the husband added.

The woman made a dismissive gesture. "Don't pay any attention to what he's saying. If you can read Spanish, find a copy of *Aboard the Caleuche* by Antonio Cardenas Tabies."

Her husband just rolled his eyes and sat back, but we made note of the book and author for future reference.

CHILOE AND THE GHOST SHIP

As soon as we arrived in Puerto Montt the next morning, we found a place to stay, a modest but comfortable B&B across the street from the water. The manager of the place directed us to a store where we could buy winter coats and also gave us the schedule for the daily ferry departures for Chiloe.

"Do you know anything about the Caleuche?" Trish asked her.

"Eerie legends," she replied with a smile. "Just folklore. But in the living room, on the bookcase, you'll find a book called *Aboard the Caleuche*. You can take it with you, if you want. It's been there for years."

It was the book the woman on the train had mentioned. Another synchronicity, we thought, and left to buy our winter coats and our ferry tickets. That evening, as a thick fog rolled in off the water, we sat on our balcony, bundled up in our coats, sipping Chilean wine and reading from *Aboard the Caleuche.*

The following morning, we hopped the ferry for Ancud, one of three towns on Chiloe, located at the northernmost part of the island. We checked into a small family-run hotel, and were surprised we were the only guests. Then again, it was the middle of winter.

We walked around the picturesque little town with its weathered wooden buildings, small, intimate shops, colorful restaurants and cafes. Everywhere you looked, the sea was usually visible—the water a shocking blue, the beaches curving gracefully along the coast, and yellow wooden fishing boats beached on shore or bobbing in the water. Fishermen with nets were visible through the mist. Sea gulls shrieked and swept in low over the beaches, stealing bits of whatever the fishermen unloaded.

On Chiloe, there's a palpable sense of the mysterious, the unseen. It's in the very salt of the air you breathe, and rides in the mist, daring you to explore it. For a couple of South Floridians accustomed to the tourist tackiness of Key West, Chiloe was another world altogether.

We found a place to eat near our hotel, on a street that sloped toward the harbor, and quickly discovered that the ghost ship wasn't just a myth to the locals. The owner of the restaurant contended that the stories are based on real events that involved encounters with the *brujos*, or witches, who allegedly manned the ship.

The island's stories were spiced with tales of mermaids that supposedly inhabited the waters near the island, with the ghost ship and its mysterious appearances in a local harbor, and with its strange crew. The legends were cultural emblems of the island, depicted on ashtrays, postcards, and wall art. Model ships of the Caleuche were complemented by figurines of the mermaids and the *brujos*, who looked like tiny men-in-black.

We asked our waiter if anyone in town had seen the Caleuche and he waved his hand toward the harbor. "Ask the fishermen down there."

After we ate, we walked down the road toward the harbor. We encountered a hunched, elderly woman wrapped in a heavy woolen poncho who moved along with the aid of a walking stick. We greeted her in Spanish and she looked us over, pegged us as tourists, then told us we should have come during the summer—in January. *"Ahora, no hay turistas aqui."* There aren't any tourists here now.

When we asked if she or anyone she knew had seen the Caleuche, she considered the question a moment. "If I did, I would not say. But talk to him." She motioned toward the same fisherman our waiter had pointed out, then moved on.

A cold breeze blew in from the harbor as we continued to the pier and then down to the beach. The fisherman was unloading his catch from one of the small, yellow wooden boats we had seen during our walk through town. It didn't look as if it would survive the waves the breeze had kicked up, much less a squall. But instead of fish, he had two large buckets filled with sea urchins.

We greeted him and he glanced up, his face as wizened as Yoda's, each wrinkle a story, an experience, a secret held. "*Buenos dias*," he said, then picked up one of the sea urchins, sliced off the spines and cut it in half. He splashed the jellylike innards with lime juice and offered us each half.

While Rob sampled the local delicacy—and then devoured it—Trish asked the fisherman about mermaids. She had grown up in Venezuela and was fluent in Spanish. The fisherman chuckled and gazed out to sea. "The legend says that when the fish are running, the mermaids face shore. When the fish are gone, the mermaids face the ocean, so their backs are to us."

"Have you ever seen a mermaid?" she asked.

He shook his head. "It's a story from long ago."

"Have you ever seen the Caleuche?"

"Me? No. But my grandfather did. And there are villagers who have seen the ship. But many are afraid to talk about it."

Fortunately, some islanders have been willing to tell their stories and Chilean author Antonio Cardenas Tabies interviewed many of them for *Aboard the Caleuche*. Like many authors who write about a particular subject, Tabies had a personal experience that intensified his interest in the Calecuhe.

Some years earlier, he and four friends were in a rowboat when they encountered a thick fog that suddenly engulfed them. A small launch approached him and his companions and even though it passed within a few feet of their boat, they never saw anyone on board or heard any noise from the motor. They kept rowing in the direction of the shore, but couldn't find land. They rowed for hours and at dawn, found themselves in the same spot they'd been when the fog had swallowed them. "We hadn't advanced a meter in any direction."

That description parallels an historical account in Massachusetts reported by John Winthrop in *The History of New England, 1630-1639*. Winthrop was governor of Massachusetts Bay Colony at the time and witnesses brought the incident to his attention. While rowing a boat on the Muddy River in Boston, several men glimpsed a bright light in the sky that "flamed up," hovered, and darted about. It remained in the sky for about three hours. When the light finally disappeared, the men were dismayed to discover that they had somehow been carried against the tide back to the place where they had started their trip. Governor Winthrop noted, "... other credible persons saw the same light, after, about the same place."

Tabies believed that the launch was the Caleuche in one of its altered forms, and as they crossed paths with it, the crew of *brujos* had cast a spell on them. Could it be that Tabies and his companions were actually abducted and only believed they had rowed all night in the same position? Loss of memory is one of the common attributes of the alien abduction scenario. Regardless, that experience enhanced Tabies' interest in the legend and led him to seek out islanders who had witnessed an appearance of the ship or encountered members of its crew.

Many of the stories Tabies recounted deal with crew members, who bear an uncanny resemblance to MIBs, and were notorious for abducting islanders. When the abductees returned to their villages, they either didn't remember or refused to talk of where they'd been. One man, who was supposedly taken at the age of 18, returned to his village fifty years later. When questioned, he simply said he had been on a boat, and implored his brother not to ask anything more about it.

Elena Vera Guerrero of Ancud met the man. "I was visiting Marcelino Saldivia, a friend who lives in another village, and took offense at the strange behavior of one of the men present. He didn't bother to say hello, practically never spoke, and seemed so remote he might as well not have been there."

Saldivia told her the man was his brother, who had disappeared half a century ago while sleeping on the porch. During Easter week 1976, Saldivia was feeling nostalgic about his lost brother and visited their old home on the banks of the Rio Pudeto. There, seated in the living room and dressed in the same clothes he'd worn as a young man, was his brother, now old and evidently demented.

Tabies told of another man, Juan Antonio Fernandez, who was 16 when he left his home at dawn one day to go fishing and was abducted by the crew of the *Caleuche*. He recalled that when he arrived at a small hill that overlooked the beach, he heard a strange humming noise, like motors. Two days later, his family found him wandering aimlessly on the beach. "I had a terrible scar on my chest, shaped like a gigantic hand with long, narrow fingers," Fernandez said. "It didn't hurt and the strange part was that it looked as if it were old."

When Tabies spoke with Fernandez's family, they said Juan was never quite the same after his disappearance. He assaulted people without provocation and spoke and worked only when he was in the mood. Tabies coaxed Fernandez, then in his sixties, into showing him his scar. "I have never seen anything like it," he said. "The hand covered almost his entire chest, like a scar from a severe burn. When I questioned him about it, he said that if he revealed the secret he would die."

Armando Pacheco, another Chilean writer, theorized that the legend of the Caleuche is so deeply ingrained in the psyche of the islanders that they are predisposed to sightings. He contended that the Caleuche is an archetype of the collective mind of the islanders, "given reality through their intense and prolonged belief in it."

The belief in the ghost ship runs so deeply through the Chiloe culture that the islanders take special care with aquatic birds and animals for fear that one of them might be a *brujo*—a sorcerer—from the ghost ship, but in an altered form. "The legend," wrote Tabies, "states that if any harm comes to a crew member while he is transformed, the guilty party will be killed or abducted and condemned to sail the seas forever as a galley slave."

One night in March 1976, a farmer in Chauques, an archipelago to the northeast of Chiloe, heard a cry that awakened him, a "kind of bleating," that seemed to be coming from under his house. He got his dogs, woke up the maid and they went outside to investigate. A wolf was trapped between some mud-wall panels. The farmer quickly unfastened three of the panels and the wolf scampered out into the darkness and toward the sea. "I have never before seen a wolf in these parts," Tabies wrote. "I have no doubt the animal was a mariner from the *Caleuche*."

When we visited the National Museum in Ancud, it was a rather humble building that housed a small, straw-woven sailing vessel, representing the ghost ship. It rested in the center of a table of the main room. Surrounding it were an assortment of straw creatures—wood nymphs, sea monsters, trolls, mermaids and *brujos,* all symbolizing the island's mythological inhabitants. Uribe Velazque, who at that time was the museum's director, believed the ghost ship exists only in the fertile imaginations of the islanders, as part of their rich folkloric tradition.

"What would Chiloe be without her Caleuche, her trolls and mermaids and sorcerers?" she wrote in an article. "I can't imagine a night of the full moon without the sudden appearance of the illuminated ghost ship. I cannot conceive of a summer twilight when the profound silence is not broken by the Caleuche's enchanted music."

Tabies, though, firmly believed the Caleuche exists. He cited Tim Dinsdale, author of *Loch Ness Monster*. "There are two types of mysteries: those which are accounts of experiences which have occurred and cannot be explained, and those born of the history of a people." The Caleuche, said Tabies, is a mystery of both kinds.

Before we left Ancud and continued our way across the island, we walked along a dirt road toward the outskirts of town. We passed a low-lying neighborhood where many of the homes were built on stilts that kept them above water when the river flooded. We paused on a bridge that crossed the Rio Pudeto and gazed out over the bay. It was here where, one night in 1968, Aaron Garcia Gonzalez, a pastor in Ancud, was startled to see a large sailing vessel enter the shallow, unnavigable waters of the Rio Pudeto. "I saw several brilliant lights, then a mast, then two more masts and finally, a ship illuminated in brilliant colors." Father Garcia watched the ship for half an hour before it faded away in the same slow manner that it had materialized.

While sighting the ship from a distance, as Father Garcia did, might be enchanting, meeting the crew face-to-face was another matter, islanders told Tabies. Like the MIBs, who have infiltrated popular culture through movies and stories of encounters, the members of the Caleuche crew sometimes come ashore and knock on doors with strange requests. Jose Barrientos, a farmer, claimed that one night in 1945 a man he believed was a crew member of the Caleuche came to his house with a message.

"He was tall and thin. He had large eyes and was dressed in a dark suit and tie and black shoes." The stranger told Barrientos that his mother, who had recently died, had found a box of china and if she had kept her discovery secret, she would have become a wealthy woman and lived to an old age. Instead, she and Barrientos' sister, brother and several friends had sold the china.

"Because of this, your mother and sister died and so will your brother." The man gave Barrientos a letter to take to another women who he said still had some of the china. Barrientos was told that if that woman didn't return the goods, she would die and so would her two sons. "You are to give her my message," the stranger instructed him. "Then you are to gather up the remaining pieces of china and leave them in the woods, where we will retrieve them."

Barrientos delivered the message to the woman the next morning.

But when her husband found out why he had come, the man turned his dogs loose on Barrientos. Shortly afterward the woman, her two sons and Barrientos' brother died, just as the stranger had predicted.

PARALLELS TO ALIEN ABDUCTIONS

This "stranger in the know" is another facet of the alien abduction experience that is sometimes mentioned by experiencers. Typically, the abductee has never seen this individual before, but the stranger has inside information about what's actually going on. The stranger offers advice, confidential information, or may deliver a threatening message.

Barrientos was convinced the deaths were a reprisal because the individuals had kept something that belonged to the Caleuche. "The rest of the people involved saved themselves by throwing the china into the sea," he said.

But why would the crew be so interested in dinnerware? Probably because the china wasn't china, but something else altogether.

According to Tabies, the crew members also occasionally make pacts with islanders who act as agents for them. If, for instance, the crew wishes to hold a celebration, the agent arranges the details. He might draw up a contract with one of the villagers, stating that in return for the use of his home and his silence, he will be rewarded with gold.

Other times, crew members confront islanders directly. Elena Guerrero's first experience with the Caleuche involved what she believed was an attempt by crew members to establish a pact. "I was young, still living with my parents at the time. Around twilight we saw a brilliantly-colored ship headed toward land. Maybe my parents realized it was the ghost ship because they sent my brothers, sisters and me off to bed. I was the only one who disobeyed. Through the window I could see seven seamen approaching the house."

When the men knocked, her father asked what they wanted. One of them replied: "Water and provisions, and for this you will be well paid in gold."

Elena heard her father tell the men he would rather be poor the rest of his life than give them even a drop of water. "To this day, I still don't understand why the mariners didn't take reprisals against my father."

While many islanders fear the sight of the Caleuche, Graciela Ruiz, a seamstress of the nearby island of Lemuy, sought out the ghost ship. She claimed that each year on the same date the ship surfaces in the Bay of Lincay near Lemuy. On this particular date in 1976 she and some friends walked to a small hill where they had a view of the bay.

"We hid behind some rocks on a hill because the mariners of the *Caleuche* can see a great distance, and there we waited. Midnight finally arrived and suddenly we saw a light rising from the depths of the water. It lit up the entire bay. A gigantic ship emerged, bright as gold, and we were so close it was like we were on board."

Ruiz says she saw an immense salon where men and women were dancing to a majestic orchestra whose music she and her friends heard clearly. The festivities lasted three or four hours, she recalled. Then just before dawn, the boat started to sink. "We watched until it vanished beneath the surface. Only then could we leave because it would have been dangerous before."

Anna Tabies Diaz, a native of the village of Huidad on Chiloe, recalled that one morning a tree trunk some 90 feet long and 18 feet wide at the base appeared in the salt marsh near her home. There had been no wind during the night that might have swept such a trunk into the marsh, and the sea didn't reach that far inland. By noon, a flock of crows had perched on the truck.

"From that day onward for the next ten years, the crows and trunk remained," Diaz said. "There were storms with high winds, but the giant trunk never moved—until one day a villager chopped into it and the trunk bled."

That same night, also windless, the trunk disappeared. Shortly afterwards the villager who had hacked into the trunk with an axe, also vanished. "I have no doubt the trunk was the Caleuche, anchored there," she said. And the crows, she contended, were the mariners.

That story, more than the others, links the ghost ship saga to one of the most mysterious aspects of the modern alien abduction scenario. Like the Caleuche, UFOs and their crew are known to shape shift. One life-long abductee you'll meet in this book found herself abducted with a rock star, who she had just seen in concert. When she angrily asked what he was doing there, the rock star shaped shifted into a Gray. That ability makes us wonder about the abductions that involve U.S. military personnel mixed with Grays. You'll read about such a case in a later chapter.

In essence, alien abductors may be archetypal tricksters who not only manipulate our view of reality, but tear it apart and leave abductees with their worldview in shreds. The abductees, like Humpty Dumpty after his fall, struggle to tape the pieces back together again and discover it's impossible. They can no longer accept reality as they once perceived it.

The UFO and alien presence fit perfectly into our high tech world as a twenty-first century mystery, a science fiction saga merging with our everyday reality. Just as in centuries past, when fairies, Djinn and other mythical creatures were said to abduct people, the residents of an isolated island in southern Chile experienced their version of the story in the form of a ghost ship and its crew. And we are experiencing ours.

Is it part of the collective unconscious being made conscious? Or is it something else entirely? What's really going on here?

In Chile, like many places in South America, the culture is more open to the possibility that myths and legends are real. In the Amazon, for instance, indigenous tribes believe that the pink dolphin is actually a shape shifter who, on the nights of the full moon, becomes a human male who wears a hat to cover his blowhole. He sneaks into the nearest village, abducts the prettiest woman, then takes her to the river, to his underwater lair, and impregnates her. Sound familiar?

When we first heard this story during the years that we led adventure tours to the Peruvian Amazon and elsewhere in South America, we laughed about it: *The dolphin did it!* We figured the story was an explanation for pregnancies out of wedlock. But the pink dolphin version of the shape shifter/abduction story bears some uncanny parallels to the tales of the Caleuche and its crew and to the alien abduction story.

In Arab countries, the abductor, the one who terrorizes the masses, is the Djinn, beings described as "master tricksters," who abduct humans for unsavory purposes. The Djinn, like the legendary Grays, try to manipulate and control their victims. They are not nice guys.

In San Augustine, Colombia, there's an archaeological park that consists of statues that are as anomalous as those on Easter Island or on the Markawasi plateau in Peru. A businessman we met during our Amazon travels described his experience in San Augustine as horrifying. He claimed he was "taken over" by several entities, spoke in some ancient language no one with him understood, and that he "was shown things" about the beings who created the statues. And, guess what? They weren't from Earth.

In North America, abductee experiences are generally written off as the result of false memories recalled under hypnosis, lucid dreaming, sleep paralysis, delusions, schizophrenia, or as a mask for childhood sexual abuse. Careers have been built on such theories. But suppose these stories, these anecdotes, are a part of something larger, part of an emerging paradigm that will be as *alien* to us now as smartphones, WiFi and the

Internet, Facebook and Twitter would have been to a resident of the 1800s?

Imagine Edgar Allan Poe with a cell phone and an iPad. Ridiculous, right?

But suppose that's the equivalent of where we humans stand now in the early twenty-first century relative to UFO encounters and alien abductions? Are we, through these tales about UFO encounters and abductions, coming face to face with an emerging new paradigm?

Like Hansel and Gretel, we're babes lost in the woods and struggle to leave a trail of breadcrumbs so that we can find our way back home to—what? The choices for Hansel and Gretel weren't exactly great. They could follow the breadcrumbs and return to their father's abusive and sadistic second wife, who wanted to lose them in the woods so she and her husband wouldn't have to share their food with them. Or, they could move on into the unknown.

Hansel and Gretel encountered a beautiful little house in the woods made of sugar and settled in. They didn't realize the house was a trap created by a cannibalistic hag who wanted to fatten them up and eat them.

Are the alien abductors *our* cannibalistic hags? Or are they our liberators? In the fairy tale, the children outwit the hag, the wicked witch, and we imagine them moving on in their lives like characters in a movie sequel that hasn't been made yet. Do they live happily ever after? Is such a thing possible for abductees?

According to many, the answer is no. Like the couple in the next chapter, abductees try to integrate their experiences into their lives and find it incredibly difficult as they repeatedly face some basic questions: *What* happened to me? *Why* did it happen? *How* do I deal with it?

CHAPTER 2

BACKYARD ENCOUNTER

One evening in late February of 2012, Charles Fontaine sat down at his computer and typed Synchronicity and UFOs into Google. The search led him to a blog post that included an illustration of a hovering UFO with a cone of light beaming down to the ground. It startled him. The image was nearly identical to what he had seen from his back porch in March 2011. Except, he had seen nine such beams moving across the field behind his house.

To the right of the blog post, he noticed the picture of a book cover, *7 Secrets of Synchronicity*. He'd just purchased that book a couple of days earlier at a Montreal bookstore. It was then he realized that the authors of the blog and book were the same, and he knew he had to contact them. Maybe they could help him understand what happened to him and his wife. So, synchronicity guided Charles Fontaine our way.

This is his story.

GRAVEYARD SNAPSHOT

Late March of 2011 in rural Quebec felt like the dead of winter. Bitter cold and impenetrable darkness wrapped around the house. Charles Fontaine decided to spend the night in the basement where his fox terrier, Spot, was already curled up on his bed in front of the wood-burning stove. He added a couple of logs to the stove, then settled down on the couch to watch *Tout le Monde en Parle*, a Quebec talk show. But Charles couldn't focus on the television screen. His mind kept drifting back to an incident that began in a graveyard nine days earlier and ended in the emergency room.

He had started a project to create a family tree and had enlisted his father's help in identifying family tombstones in their hometown cemetery. When they arrived, the wind was whipping through the graveyard, and clumps of crusty snow clung to the frozen turf. While his father located specific tombstones, Charles jotted down the birth and death dates on three sheets of paper that listed family names. But a chilling gust of wind came up, making it difficult to write. He backtracked to the car for his digital camera and began snapping photos of gravestones.

One of his father's brothers had been buried in the cemetery on Feb. 19, 2011, exactly a month earlier. Charles and his father didn't attend the funeral because of a family dispute dating back to 1984. It involved a family business and was serious enough that it had to be settled in court. It was very difficult for his father not go to the funeral, but it would have been uncomfortable with other hostile family members in attendance.

While Charles was snapping photos, his father, across the graveyard, suddenly caught his breath, tensed, and looked around. He sensed a malign presence nearby, and felt a nearly overpowering urge to flee. A voice seemed to whisper in his head. *Tell your son to get away from there. Get him away quickly.* He shouted for Charles, yelled as loudly as he could, but the wind seemed to swallow his voice.

Charles remembered hearing his father calling to him. At the time, he was photographing the family tombstone where his recently deceased uncle was buried, and hurried away from the grave and looked for his father. Oddly, Charles had trouble finding him.

That evening, Charles drove Bridgette, his 17-year-old daughter, to a nearby city for her part-time job at a restaurant. On the way, he felt a stabbing pain in his stomach and began sweating profusely. He felt wetness in his pants and pulled into a gas station. Embarrassed, he hurried to the restroom, thinking that he had urinated on himself. It was worse. Blood filled his pants.

His first thought was that he was going to die. His father had had colon cancer twenty years earlier, but was saved by surgery. Now, Charles thought, it was his turn. Filled with dread, he dropped his daughter off at work, then drove to the emergency room and was examined by a physician. At his recommendation, Charles made an appointment with a doctor who specialized in colon surgery.

He was still confused about what had happened that day and worried that he might require immediate surgery. He returned his focus to the television where the host was questioning a politician. A while later, Bridgette came downstairs, said good night and went to her bedroom. Charles turned off the lights and the television. He put more logs into the stove and settled back down on the couch. He would see the surgeon at 8:30 in the morning. Within a few minutes, he fell asleep.

FIELD OF BEAMS

At 3 a.m., Charles came awake at the sound of shouts from upstairs. His wife sounded angry, but about what? Alarmed, he bolted off the couch to see what was going on—and noticed that Spot was no longer on his bed. He hurried up the stairs and headed to the master bedroom. The lights blazed and Helene was standing beside the bed, shouting at the dog to get down.

Spot, teeth bared, had assumed an aggressive stance on the bed and refused to obey. They'd never seen him act this way. It was clear that something was wrong with him. Charles finally enticed the dog with a treat and lured him off the bed and back downstairs to the basement. He shut the door, stretched out on the couch, and dozed off.

Charles' normal routine in the morning was to get up by 5 a.m., let the dog outside, then feed him when he returned. Usually, he woke his daughter at 5:30 and they drove into the city together, where Charles worked and his daughter attended college. But this morning was disturbingly different.

At 4:50 a.m., he was awakened again by Spot, whimpering. *Now what?* He sat up and saw the dog standing in front of the wood stove, trembling and shaking and looking toward a window on the southeast side of the house. The dog wasn't the least bit interested in going outside. He just stood there, shaking, his attention fixed on the window.

Charles walked over to Spot and gently touched his side to comfort him. An odd thought came to mind: he felt that Spot was going to die soon. After awhile, Spot calmed down and followed Charles upstairs. He walked to the patio door, which faces east, and reached down for the dog's leash.

That was when he noticed beams of light, very low in intensity, in the expansive field behind the house. He opened the patio door, but the dog refused to go out. Charles grabbed him, forced him out, and shut the door. As Spot passed the motion detector sensor, the patio spotlights came on, illuminating the backyard. Charles couldn't see the beams any longer so he hit the switch, turning off the lights. After a few seconds, his eyes adjusted and he saw the beams of light again.

Now they burned with greater intensity and seemed to be moving closer and closer to his backyard. He counted nine distinct beams shaped like inverted ice cream cones, displayed asymmetrically across the field. They looked brighter near the ground and lost intensity toward the top. Some glowed more powerfully than others. He couldn't see anything above the cones except darkness. He didn't have any idea what he was looking at.

At first, he thought these cones might be solid acrylic tubes that were illuminated. He could even see movement inside the beams, like heat waves rising off a road surface on a scorching summer day. Whatever they were, Charles thought they were beautiful and was paralyzed by the spectacle. He watched for a couple minutes, then retreated and called out to Helene. "Are you awake?"

She mumbled that she was.

"I want you to see something. I want to know if you see the same thing that I do."

Helene hurried out of the bedroom and over to the patio door and looked out the window. "Wow, what is it, pyrotechnics?" she asked. "This is exactly what I saw the other day! I told you about it, remember?"

Charles vaguely recalled her talking about an incident that scared her while she was driving. And now, distracted by the display in front of them, he lost track of what his wife was saying. A vertical tube—something different from the beams of light—hung just above the weeping willow tree to the right side of their backyard. For a few seconds, it glowed as brightly as lightning, then went dark, then reappeared. This same thing happened over and over again, the brilliant glow, the darkness, the glow again. He couldn't turn away from it.

"Helene, do you see that one to the right?" he asked, catching his breath.

She didn't respond.

He was amazed, mesmerized, but not fearful. Gradually, he detected something at one side of the vertical tube, a gray metallic structure, a craft of some sort. It was saucer-shaped and turned sideways, like a coin balanced on its rim. On the last two illuminations, he saw something even more baffling: beads of bright white lights, shaped like O-rings or Cheerios, that floated in the tube. The tube itself now appeared as a luminous blue, the O-rings bright white.

He wrenched his eyes away, opened the patio door, leaned out and called for Spot. Even though it was dark, he saw the dog clearly surrounded by a beam of yellow light. And that's the last thing Charles remembered. The next thing he knew, he was in the shower, shampooing his hair.

He had no idea how he'd gotten there or how much time had passed. His head hammered and throbbed from an excruciating pressure, as though he had the mother of all hangovers. He was confused, but not afraid. The fear would come later.

He shaved, dried his hair, brushed his teeth, did it all on automatic. Then he returned to the patio. It was still dark out, but the beams of light were gone. He didn't even bother to look in the bedroom for Helene. He just knew she was there. He left with Bridgette on time, at 5:30, and drove to the city. He arrived at work at 7 a.m., right on time.

FEAR AND DEPRESSION

Once Charles was inside his office, alone, the door closed, he simply stared at the floor and struggled with the excruciating pressure in his head, the terrible aching in his eyes. He knew something was profoundly wrong. Nothing made sense. One moment he had been standing at the patio door, then he was in the shower. Not much time could've passed. Yet, something had happened, he was sure of it. But he couldn't remember what. It was as if time had expanded, then contracted, and he had been caught inside, taken, then returned to his own time frame.

"I was forty-nine years old and I started to cry," Charles recalled.

At that moment, he began to realize that he and Helene had experienced something that was not supposed to exist, that had never existed for him until earlier that morning. He'd never been interested in UFOs, aliens, any of it. Such things were only a celluloid reality, Hollywood fiction. He assumed UFOs were just ordinary objects mistakenly identified as alien spacecraft. "I thought that if UFOs existed, the Americans—NASA, the army, air force, you name it—would have told us long ago."

And yet, he knew what he had seen. He suspected that he'd been abducted, and it terrified him.

At the doctor's appointment that morning, Charles felt distracted, unsettled, still scared. "While I waited for my appointment with the specialist, I kept thinking it was all only a dream, a bad dream, that it was impossible. It could not be real. I moved away from everyone else, looked down at the floor and cried."

His appointment was brief, a colonoscopy was scheduled and he was given a prescription to take the day before he returned. He went back to work and remained behind a closed door and cried again. The longer he sat in his office, the more frightened and depressed he became.

Charles felt as if he had been abused and controlled against his will. They—whatever *they* were—had made the rules. They had allowed him to wake up his wife, but had controlled the game. Deep inside, he desperately wanted to scream and let people know *they* exist. But he doubted anyone would listen, that anyone would believe him. He felt trapped in a new reality that no one would accept. He wished he had never been born. He even contemplated suicide.

Exhausted, he did the minimum amount of work required, then left the office early. He picked up his daughter at college and started home.

Bridgette wasn't aware of what had happened earlier in the day. He hadn't told her, didn't want to scare her. During the drive, she talked about her day at school, but he wasn't listening. He couldn't concentrate. "I felt a constant pressure in my head and all I wanted to do was cry."

Finally, she turned to him and frowned. "What's wrong with you, Dad? Are you crying?"

As soon as they arrived home, Charles walked over to the patio door and looked through the window. He tried to gauge the distance that the circular object—what he thought of as *the machine*—had been from the house before he blacked out. It had been blinking off and on and moving closer and closer. Now, he figured it had been about 150 feet away.

He stepped into the kitchen where Helene was preparing dinner. As she met his gaze, he said: *"Et alors?"* And so?

She looked confused, at a loss as to what he was referring to, as if she already had forgotten what happened, or couldn't quite remember. *"Et alors quoi?"* And so what?

At that point, he was afraid her memory had been wiped clean and he was the only one who remembered, and that made it all even more frightening. *"Tu sais ce matin...ce matin lorsque je suis allé te reveiller!"* And this morning...this morning when I woke you up!

The look on her face changed instantly. "That was very special," she said quietly.

"What was special?"

"The beams of light. The energy rising inside the cones. All the colors. All that energy at the bottom of the cones. It was all so special. It was getting brighter and brighter and was being pulled upward toward the top of the cones."

"Do you remember hearing me ask you to look on the right side? Do you remember my saying, 'Do you see the tube...can you see it?'"

She replied that she remembered hearing him, but had been too fascinated by the beams of light out in the field to reply. "Five beams," she said. "I counted five of them." Helene remembered feeling hypnotized or paralyzed, then nothing. She didn't recall how long she had stood there, watching the beams, or how she had gotten to the bedroom. She felt as if she had floated through the air and had been placed gently on the mattress.

Instantly, she felt like she weighed a ton, and it seemed the mattress had wrapped around her completely. She fell asleep and woke up as usual at 7 a.m.

She told Charles she felt rested, which she found unusual because her sleep had been interrupted twice by odd events. She had no problem getting to work on time.

Then, suddenly, a cloud seemed to clear from her mind. "Wait, don't you remember? I told you that I had seen this same thing once before."

Now Charles was confused and asked her to explain. Two weeks ago, she said, she recalled standing beside her car, watching those same cones of light. She remembered wishing Charles and Bridgette were with her to see the spectacle. He asked where she had been when it had happened.

"I don't know exactly. But I got home around 8:30 and I told you that something scared me while I was driving. But you weren't paying any attention to what I was saying."

Charles vaguely recalled the conversation. But he thought she'd been talking about a deer crossing the road in front of her. "You are always afraid of deer, so I didn't bother listening closely."

Then she seemed to recall more. "I was alone on this country road that I take every day, and you know me, I always drive safely, keeping an eye out for deer that might jump out in front of my car. Suddenly, this strange reflection appeared on my windshield. It was shaped like a inverted muffin mold with three inlaid red dials."

She had realized that the reflection wasn't from something within the car, but from an object outside of it. Then she sensed a huge bright light moving rapidly toward her. "I instantly closed my eyes and my whole body tensed. I was terrified. I expected to be hit by something. And for a moment, I thought that was it."

Then she had opened her eyes and looked to her left, the side from which she'd seen the light. She clearly glimpsed about thirty deer lying in a field. They weren't dead, because they were lifting their heads, struggling to stand. But why were they lying down? She thought it might be related to a lightning strike or to something going on at the army base a couple of miles away.

The next thing she remembered was standing somewhere on a road, but she had no idea where. "I was alone, outside of my car, watching those cones of light, exactly the same thing we both saw this morning."

Charles wondered what her experience meant and why she hadn't said more about it earlier. "What if I hadn't asked you about what happened this morning, Helene?"

"Then I probably would've forgotten everything," she replied.

A while later, they all sat down at the table for dinner. Charles wasn't hungry and started to complain about the constant pressure in his head. He was extremely depressed. Spot didn't seem well, either. He hadn't come to Charles as he usually did when he arrived home from work. The dog stayed on the bed in the bedroom, gazing toward the patio door in the other room. Helene remarked that Spot hadn't gone outside since morning.

Their daughter thought they were acting strangely and asked what was wrong with them. They blamed it on the dog not feeling well and waking them up early in the morning.

After dinner, Charles wanted to go behind the house to the field and take a look around. But it was already getting dark, and he was afraid to step outside. Darkness had taken on a whole new meaning.

Charles and Helene stayed up late talking about their experience. As he tried to articulate his fear, he started crying again and Helene comforted him. It surprised him that she wasn't afraid or shocked like he was. She even told him: "You know, what happened to us is exactly as if we had won the lottery. We were lucky enough to see something that others will probably never see in their entire lives. But the difference between winning the lottery and what we saw is that you can prove to people that you won the lottery by showing them the winning ticket. But with our experience, we have no proof and have no choice but to remain quiet about it."

As the evening wore on, Charles grew increasingly depressed and anxious. He felt connected to something that hadn't existed for him the day before. That night, he bunked in the basement again, on the couch, a baseball bat within easy reach. He woke up every hour and cried throughout the night. His life had collapsed into a nightmare.

ALONE, BUT NOT ALONE

Charles Fontaine's agonized reaction to the dramatic encounter, his loss of memory and subsequent despair, could be symptomatic of post-traumatic stress syndrome. Up to that point in his life, aliens and UFOs were no more real to him than vampires and fire-breathing dragons.

When we talked to him on Skype, he recalled that he thought he might be going insane. His beliefs about what was real had been altered drastically; he'd been *converted* against his will and that deeply angered and terrified him and nearly silenced him completely. The only person he could confide in was his wife, and thank God she had seen what he had, and remembered.

"I think I was more frightened than Helene, because she did not see what I saw. She focused on the energy beams in the cones of light. But I had seen the tube hanging in the air with the 0-rings, which was something altogether different. I knew it was a machine, a vehicle, from outside this world– a UFO in my own backyard."

Even after more than a year, Charles remained extremely cautious about the subject. He wanted people to know, yet feared publicly identifying himself as an experiencer. He was worried that he'd been abducted, worried because he had no memory of what happened after he blacked out.

As you'll see later, some of the events that occurred in the days and weeks after the encounter were as bizarre as the encounter itself. "If I came out into the open, I would be depicted as a clown, an idiot, a weirdo. I could even lose my job."

TRAUMA

Hollywood loves trauma. It sells tickets. *The 4400*, a TV show that ran on CBS for four seasons, from 2004-2007, focused on a group of 4400 individuals who had disappeared in a white beam of light at various times since 1946. None of the 4400 had aged from the time of their disappearance. Confused and disoriented, they remember nothing between the time of their disappearance and their return. Sounds familiar, doesn't it?

A number of researchers have written about the trauma involved in UFO encounters and abductions. Imagine, you're literally snatched out of your comfort zone—often taken right out of your bed—and hurled into some new place where you're clueless about the rules of engagement. In this new place, what constitutes reality? Are you really experiencing what you think you are? Are you really naked and paralyzed and voiceless on a table in a sterile room, surrounded by, well, *aliens?*

That's how the human mind works. Confronted by what it doesn't immediately understand, by what doesn't *compute,* the mind either spins possible explanations or it simply shuts down, incapable of doing anything at all.

In his book *Abduction: Human Encounters with Aliens*, the late John E. Mack, former professor of psychiatry at Harvard Medical School, delineated the types of trauma abductees face. "First, there's the experience itself. To be paralyzed and taken against one's will by strange beings into a foreign enclosure and subjected to intrusive, rape-like procedures, some of which are especially humiliating to human dignity, is obviously highly disturbing. In this light, it's surprising that abductees as a group are not more emotionally troubled than they are."

Second, abductees feel a lifelong sense of isolation and estrangement from other people. They learn not to talk about their experiences.

Third, as the reality of their experiences sink in, Mack believed the abductees suffer "ontological shock," a state of mind where they are forced to question their worldview. As one abductee wrote us: "Experiencers can't *unknow* what they know. Once your worldview has been turned inside out by such a shock, there's no undoing it. The fact that there are no answers (yet) for these experiences makes it even harder."

On March 28, 2011, Charles Fontaine experienced what Mack had written about years earlier. As the day unfolded, it became clear that he was profoundly traumatized. The ensuing events in days that followed (described in chapter 6) were like a psychic hangover and only magnified his angst.

Abduction related traumas, wrote Mack, "are unusual in that they can recur at any time." They aren't finite. They stick to you like Velcro.

CHAPTER 3
THE GATHERING

In South Florida, March is usually a pleasant month. The scorching heat of summer hasn't arrived yet and mornings are still cool, with a gradual warming to the mid-seventies by afternoon. March 15, 1986, was that kind of day. The temperature was in the low sixties and traffic on I-95 flowed south beneath a vast panorama of cerulean blue sky. The tourist season would be in full swing until Easter, two weeks away, then the snowbirds would return north.

During the twenty-minute drive from our place in Fort Lauderdale to a UFO conference in Hollywood, we went over our list of questions for the featured speakers—famed abductee Betty Hill and author and UFO investigator Budd Hopkins. The editor with whom we worked at OMNI Magazine was interested in articles on both of them.

At that time, OMNI was a unique entity among magazines, a slick bimonthly launched by Kathy Keeton, the long time companion and later the wife of *Penthouse* publisher Bob Guccione. In other words, it had plenty of financial backing. In the first issue, Guccione described the magazine as *"an original if not controversial mixture of science fact, fiction, fantasy and the paranormal."* It featured outstanding speculative and science fiction by writers who are now practically household names—Joyce Carol Oates, Orson Scott Card, William S. Burroughs, T. Coraghessan Boyle, even Stephen King. The magazine published an excerpt from King's *The Firestarter*.

In the nonfiction area, they published articles on technology and cutting edge ideas. One the most interesting pieces they published was on Robert Monroe, whose book, *Journeys Out of Body*, launched the Monroe Institute, where participants are guided through an exploration of consciousness, using techniques that Monroe developed. According to Monroe's stepdaughter, Nancy McMoneagle, that OMNI piece put the Monroe Institute on the map.

Our editor was interested in pieces for OMNI's Anti-Matter section, where articles about UFOs and the paranormal were featured. We were fledgling freelance writers who were delighted to get the assignment. Not only did it give us an opportunity to explore topics that interested us, but the magazine paid well and on time and even paid a one hundred percent 'kill fee' for articles they had bought but never used.

We had read *The Interrupted Journey*, John Fuller's account of the abduction of Betty and Barney Hill on September 19, 1961. We had brought our copy along for her to autograph. The Hills' experience is considered to be the beginning of what the late John E. Mack called "the modern history of abductions" and is probably one of the most famous and controversial cases in ufology. These days, a Google search for Betty and Barney Hill delivers nearly a million hits. But in 1986, there was no Google, no Internet, and the investigation of alien abductions was still relatively new.

We also had read Budd Hopkins' 1981 book *Missing Time*, the first book of its kind to map particular patterns of behavior among abductees. Missing time and screen memories were two such patterns.

Missing time usually involves the sighting of a light in the sky, then the abductee finds himself miles from where he last remembered being, it's hours later, and he can't recall what he did during those hours. Screen memories are when an abductee recalls seeing certain types of birds (owls are common) or animals (deer) or even small children in unusual places, like the bedroom. Or the abductee recalls a detailed sequence of events that has nothing to do with aliens or the abduction.

In his book, Hopkins made some rather alarming speculations—that cuts, scoops, and unexplained body scars might be part of the abduction experience. And, even worse, some abductees had implants inserted into them, and may have experienced lifelong abductions.

BETTY HILL AND BUDD HOPKINS

The conference, sponsored by a New Age bookstore, wasn't well publicized and only attracted about a hundred people. The size made it easy for attendees and speakers to mingle comfortably.

Betty was the first speaker and certainly didn't need notes for her talk. In her soft, gravelly voice, she described how on that cold September night in 1961, she and Barney were on their way home from a vacation in Canada. Betty, then a 41-year-old social worker and Barney, a 39-year-old postal worker, were driving along Route 3 through the White Mountains of New Hampshire to Portsmouth, where they lived. Around 10:15 p.m., they noticed a bright light moving erratically in the sky. They watched the light as they drove. Barney supposedly tried to convince himself that the light was an airplane, Betty thought it might be a communication satellite.

When they reached Indian Head, Barney stopped the car and got out for a closer look at the object through his binoculars. He saw lights of many colors and rows of windows on the object, which now moved toward him. When it got to within a hundred feet of him, he could see occupants inside. Terrified, he ran back to the car where Betty waited and they sped away.

On their journey home, they suddenly realized they were thirty-five miles from where they had been moments ago. They arrived home at dawn, exhausted, and only later did they recognize the fact that they couldn't account for at least two hours. A trip that should have taken them four hours had taken more than six.

In person, Betty was warm, funny, and hyper, constantly moving about and puffing on one cigarette after another. Her hands moved continually and sometimes trembled. She had a lot of nervous ticks in her facial expressions. She was 67 then, Barney had been dead for seventeen years, and she had traveled to the conference with a close friend. She talked about her experience with passion and resolve, answered questions, and all the while, her pale blue eyes flicked from the crowd to the windows and back again.

After Betty's talk, we were sitting outside with her and her companion and scheduled a time for an interview for OMNI. Just then, Budd Hopkins joined us. He had been on a radio show that morning and one of the calls was from a woman in Lake Worth, who claimed she had been abducted from her home the previous December. She had provided enough details to convince Hopkins that her story deserved further investigation. Since he hadn't rented a car, we offered to drive him to the woman's home.

During the 43-mile drive, Hopkins talked about some of the material that would be in his next book, *Intruders*—specifically the sexual experimentation many abductees reported that seemed to be related to reproduction. "In other words," Hopkins said, "these aliens are removing eggs from women and sperm from men. They're harvesting."

Some years later, David Jacobs, a Temple University historian who has hypnotically regressed more than a thousand abductees, many of them sent to him by Hopkins and other pioneers who were researching this phenomenon, expanded on Hopkins' findings. Jacobs identified urological and gynecological procedures that were performed on abductees, the presentation of infants and small children, and sexual activities, where abductees were forced to have sex with other abductees.

"Harvesting for what? Why?" Rob asked.

Hopkins shook his head. "Who knows? For cross breeding? To create a race of hybrids?"

Eight years after this drive with Hopkins, John Mack published *Abduction*, one of the most comprehensive books about the phenomenon. He described these procedures that Hopkins mentioned, where "instruments are used to penetrate virtually every part of the abductees' bodies." In addition to removing sperm from men and eggs from women, "abductees experience being impregnated by the alien beings and later having an alien-human or human-human pregnancy removed." During subsequent abductions, the abductees may see incubators where the hybrid babies are living or may be asked to hold the babies.

Intuitively, Hopkins knew he was onto something, that he had recognized vitally important patterns in the abduction phenomenon. He felt that the woman who had called into the radio show might reveal, under hypnosis, additional pieces of that pattern. He also mentioned that he'd been working with a famous author whose abduction experiences spanned many years. "He's writing the book now. And I'm telling you, when this book is published, it'll be explosive."

We pressed him for the name of the writer, but Hopkins wouldn't tell us. We figured it out less than a year later, when in February 1987, William Morrow published Whitley Strieber's *Communion*. It was a harrowing account of the writer's abduction experiences that spanned more than a decade.

Since Strieber was a popular and successful writer of fiction like *The Hunger* and *Wolfen*, he was accused of writing fiction as though it were fact, was ridiculed for his description of rectal probes, and was reviled by skeptics. The book hit the *New York Times* bestseller list and got mixed reviews. His fiction career suffered and he eventually lost his home in upstate New York where the abductions had occurred.

But Strieber persevered, continued to write and publish fiction and nonfiction and as of 2013 has one of the most comprehensive websites about the abduction scenario, ETs, and alternate realities.

On this early afternoon in March of 1986, though, all of that lay in the future. We were just three people en route to a Lake Worth home where a woman claimed to have been abducted by aliens.

HOPKINS REGRESSES AN ABDUCTEE

Since its incorporation in 1911, the city of Lake Worth has covered less than seven square miles in Palm Beach County. Today there are more than 37,000 residents, including a large Finnish population, and artists have discovered beauty in its old downtown buildings and neighborhoods. But back in 1986, it was a sleepy place inhabited mostly by retirees.

The Bristols were no doubt unlike any other couple in Lake Worth. Joe was a former Baptist minister, five or six years older than his wife, in his early forties. He sported a mane of silver hair that fell over his collar, dressed completely in black, and wore a necklace with a gold devil head dangling from it. When Rob asked him about the odd pendant, he explained that he had 'switched sides.' He talked incessantly, rarely giving his wife a chance to get in a word.

But Carol had plenty to say after Hopkins had hypnotized her. She recalled being floated from her bed, through a wall, and into a transparent tube that transported her into the starlit sky. While rising in the tube, she looked down at a huge Christmas tree displayed on the property of the nearby headquarters of the *National Enquirer*, which at that time was famous for publishing UFO stories. The tree was fully lit and Carol pointed it out to the aliens. Hopkins matter-of-factly asked how they reacted, and Carol, speaking in a soft monotone replied, "They don't react. They aren't impressed." (Our editor at OMNI loved that line in our article. "Oh, the irony!" she wrote in accepting the story.)

During the regression, Joe watched closely, occasionally fingering the devil head around his neck. While Carol and her son were gentle and sweet, Joe was imposing. We kept exchanging glances, wondering what was up with Joe, but Hopkins seemed to ignore him, as if he didn't figure into the scenario, and just focused on Carol's experiences.

We later puzzled over Carol's situation. She seemed dominated in her daily life by her peculiar husband. Then little Grays abducted her, controlled her, and abused her. We couldn't help but wonder if the abduction scenario had been a psychological event, a metaphor for her life. Yet, Hopkins was convinced that the event had taken place in the physical world. We listened to the tape of the compelling regression we had witnessed, and decided that it might be both.

Carol had awakened during the night to find three small beings at the foot of her bed. They resembled little kids. She wondered how they had gotten into her bedroom and why they were just standing there. They didn't speak, didn't move. Then suddenly she was paralyzed, still breathing but unable to move even her little finger. Yet, her mind raced with shock. She was fully aware, incredulous, and terrified. She knew something horribly disturbing and frightening beyond words, was happening to her.

As she was floated upward, her husband remained stone still on the bed, in a sleep like death. The Christmas tree was the last familiar thing she consciously remembered before disappearing into the vessel.

Under hypnosis, she described being placed on a table. Her clothes were gone, she didn't recall removing them. A taller entity hovered over her, studying her. It bent over, its head close to hers, its black eyes peering into hers. She felt it was invading her mind, her soul, her very being. She thought of her ten-year-old son asleep in the house and despaired that she might never see him again.

The tall entity held a metallic instrument in its hand and forced it into her nose and sinuses. She tried to scream, but couldn't move, couldn't make a sound. The entity spoke to her, its lips not moving, and told her to stop struggling, that it would be over soon. He stepped to the other end of the table and Carol felt a cold instrument penetrating her genitals, moving deeply inside her. She didn't know how long the procedure lasted, and had no memory of leaving the craft.

When she woke in the morning, she was in her own bed, felt bruised, abused, profoundly depressed—and didn't know why. Carol, like Betty Hill, didn't remember what had happened to her until the memories began to return to her first in dreams. Then she heard Budd Hopkins on the radio, describing alien abductions, and she became extremely nervous and uneasy. She knew without a doubt that something eerily similar had happened to her. She called the radio station and talked to Hopkins on the air. In recalling bits and pieces of her experience, she had a difficult time controlling her emotions.

Before leaving, we walked out into the Bristol's small backyard where Carol had said the tube had first appeared. Hopkins looked around, gazed up at the night sky. "Yeah, there would be enough room back here," he said.

Hopkins stayed overnight with the Bristols and when we left, we were glad *we* weren't staying.

Earlier at the conference, Hopkins had dismissed the idea that he might be an abductee himself. Out there in the Bristol's backyard, Rob asked, "Budd, do you think your work with abductees has affected your art?"

He stood there, quiet a moment, then said, "I hope not."

In spite of his comment, we had the sense that Hopkins had long since realized that his life as a respected Manhattan artist was taking second place to his life as an author and abduction investigator. In his memoir, *Art, Life and UFOs*, published in 2004, he talks about this dichotomy in his life. He also notes that someone had asked him if he believed UFOs really existed and if the thousands of accounts by abductees were actually true. "I recall answering, sadly, I no longer had the luxury of *dis*belief. Even back in the 1970s I felt the sense of being helpless in the face of the accumulating evidence, and aware that the UFO phenomenon made the future seem increasingly ominous."

He went on to establish the Intruders Foundation, continued to regress abductees, and to collect information that resulted in several other books. The following year, in fact, his book *Intruders* was published and became a *New York Times* bestseller.

AN EVENING WITH BETTY HILL

We returned to the conference the next day for an interview with Betty Hill. We invited Betty and her friend to our townhouse in Fort Lauderdale, and they agreed to join us that evening.

We were somewhat embarrassed when the four of us entered our place, what with dust bunnies hiding under the TV and stereo, and books and files cluttering tabletops and spilling onto the floor. But neither Betty nor her friend seemed to notice.

We put together a platter of veggies, cheese, and fruit, brought out some beer, and sat in the living room, where Betty entertained us with stories about all the UFO sightings she'd had since she and Barney were abducted. Once Betty was talking, there was no interrupting her. She was in the flow, out there, *gone.*

She was an affable woman with a quick laugh and a terrific sense of humor. But when she started talking about what had happened to her and Barney, the mirth bled away. Her eyes seemed haunted, particularly as she described the details. There were eleven Grays. She referred to one of them as the leader, because he seemed to be in charge and was the only one who "spoke English." Then there was the examiner, the Gray who conducted the physical tests, and nine other crew members.

She and Barney were examined in separate rooms. Under hypnosis several years after their experience, they both reported that the examiner took samples of their hair, fingernails, and skin, examined their eyes, nose, throat, ears, and tested their nervous systems. Barney recalled that sperm was taken from him. When Betty's examiner brought out an instrument with a long needle and Betty was told he was going to insert it into her navel, she was beyond terrified. "I wanted to know what they were about to do to me. The leader explained it was a pregnancy test. I told him it would hurt…" But the examiner inserted the needle despite her protests and she squirmed in agony until the leader touched Betty's forehead and the pain went away.

At one point Betty seemed overwhelmed by her memories and abruptly pushed her chair back from the table, stood, and made a beeline for the sliding glass doors, opened them, and vanished outside. The rest of us hurried after her and found Betty in the middle of the parking lot in front of our townhouse, arm moving slowly, finger pointed skyward, following a light. "See that?" she exclaimed. "See that light?"

We glanced at each other, both of us thinking the same thing. The lights came from a plane. But it was Betty's friend who voiced the obvious.

"No," Betty said with a shake of her head. "They can camouflage themselves. They're masters of camouflage."

Well, maybe they are, who can say for sure? But the point wasn't the light—plane, satellite, UFO— it was that she uttered this statement with the same resolve we had noticed during her passionate talk at the conference.

"When Barney and I…what we experienced, what we saw…what happened…" She talked in fits and starts, as if she couldn't spit the words out quickly enough.

And suddenly, standing out there in the parking lot beneath a sky strewn with stars, any doubts we had about Betty Hill vanished. Utterly. Completely. This woman and her husband had experienced *something* out there on Route 3, on September 19, 1961. But *what?*

Whatever it was, the event sculpted the rest of Betty's life. Because of Fuller's book, a subsequent article in *Look* Magazine, and then a movie, she and Barney became internationally known as the first modern day UFO abductees. Rather than hiding her experience, Betty spoke out and expressed the collective experience of those who came later.

The procedure Betty described—the needle through her navel—sounds similar to amniocentesis. During an amniocentesis, a small amount of fluid is taken from the amniotic sac surrounding a developing fetus and the fetal DNA is examined for genetic abnormalities. The gender of the fetus can also be determined. But this procedure wasn't known in 1961 and didn't come into widespread use until the late 1980s.

Both Betty and Barney suffered from nightmares and profound anxiety in the aftermath of their experience. In late 1963, they underwent hypnotic regression with Benjamin Simon, a physician in Boston. During one session, Dr. Simon gave Betty a post hypnotic suggestion that she could sketch a copy of the three dimensional "star map" she had seen on the ship. She eventually did so and drew twelve prominent stars that stood out in her memory, with three smaller, dimmer stars. The stars were connected by lines and dashes. The solid lines, Betty said, were trade routes. The dashes represented routes to less traveled stars.

In 1968, an elementary school teacher and amateur astronomer, Marjorie Fish, decided to decipher Betty's star map to see if it was possible to determine the star system from which the UFO originated. She constructed a three-dimensional model of nearby sun-like stars using thread and beads. It wasn't until 1969, when the Gliese Star Catalogue was published, that she was able to make a determination.

The Gliese is a modern star catalogue of stars located within 25 parsecs of Earth. One parasec is roughly 3.26 light years or about 19 trillion miles. So Fish, after studying thousands of vantage points, decided the one that seemed to be the best match was from a double star system, Zeta Reticuli. Fish concluded that the UFO that abducted the Hills may have originated from a planet orbiting Zeta Reticuli.

That night at our condo, Betty mentioned Zeta Reticuli just briefly, almost in passing. She was focused on that light in the sky, that camouflaged craft, and how she knew it was a UFO, that it was *them,* keeping an eye on her.

Most scientists, Carl Sagan among them, dismissed Fish's research and map. But Walter Mitchell, an astronomer and professor at Ohio State University, believed Fish's calculations were correct. In the December 1974 issue of *Astronomy Magazine*, he said: "The pattern discovered by Marjorie Fish has an uncanny resemblance to the map drawn by Betty Hill. The stars are mostly ones that we would visit if we were exploring from Zeta Reticuli. The travel patterns make sense."

SECOND VISIT WITH THE ABDUCTEE

We were curious about how the Bristols—Carol in particular—fared in the months after her hypnotic regression. We had spoken to them by phone several times and we finally invited them to our place for dinner. We should have guessed that doing so would attract more high strangeness.

We decided to make it a small dinner party with a few others who were interested in the abduction scenario. Among them were Renie Wiley, a psychic and empath who worked with local police on the Adam Walsh case, and Tony Grosso, with whom Rob later co-authored *The Rainbow Oracle*, a book of color divination. Only Renie had experienced UFO encounters.

Carol and her husband arrived early. Once again, Joe wore black and that gold satanic symbol hung around his neck. He was strangely quiet that night, and seemed out of his element, wary of everyone. He never moved from his chair—not to stretch, not to use the bathroom. Carol talked a little about her abduction, but mostly we just sat around talking and having a good time. Except for Joe.

Around 1 a.m., while we were talking about MIBs, men in black –not the Tommy Lee Jones movies, which didn't come out until years later—the unexpected happened. Rob glanced over at the sliding glass doors leading from the living room to a small porch and the parking lot, and there, on the porch, peering in at us, was a man dressed in dark clothing. By the time Rob alerted everyone else, the man had moved away.

Rob ran to the doors, slid them open, and could hardly believe what he saw. The man, instead of simply disappearing into the darkness beyond the parking lot, was making a scene of his escape. Crouching low, he darted from car to car like a cat, and kept glancing back at us, hiding in full view.

Trish called the police and the response astounded us. Within a few minutes, five or six patrol cars arrived, sirens shrieking, and cops with dogs spread out across the complex, searching for the man. We were baffled by the response to the relatively minor incident until we discovered that someone had been murdered an hour earlier, less than a mile away, and the killer was on the loose.

As far as we know, they never found the man *we* reported, and we don't know if he had anything to do with the murder. But it was a strange ending for an unusual evening, and we never saw the Bristols again.

The next day, Renie called to tell us what she thought of the Bristols. She believed that Carol's story was legit. They had apparently talked at one point in the kitchen, away from the rest of us. Renie also suspected that Joe's involvement in the "dark arts" may have attracted these negative entities.

We knew what Renie meant. But is it that simple?

THE MAKING OF AN ABDUCTEE

John Mack noted in *Abduction* that efforts to characterize abductees as a group haven't been successful. "They seem to come, as if at random, from all parts of society." And even now, eighteen years after the publication of his book, that statement apparently still holds true.

We asked Diane Fine, a lifelong abductee mentioned in the introduction, why she thought she had been taken. "It seems to me that some humans are marked and the answer is part of a larger view that encompasses something bigger than one lifetime. I now view these abduction experiences as just one form of my lifetime of psychic experiences. I have also seen other types of beings. Some angelic, some demonic and a wide range in between. It also seems that being human is something the Grays don't get to do, and they desperately want to 'grok' us. They are obsessed with why we are attracted to other beings: mates, pets, children, even rock idols. Our nature to feel desire seems to interest them."

Diane's comment about being 'marked' is echoed by another lifelong abductee, Jennifer White, a freelance writer and illustrator. Jennifer grew up on military bases, lives on one now, so her abduction experiences often occur on or near military bases and may involve military personnel. She refers to such abductions with a military link as 'The Program.'

"Abductees aren't chosen because of their ancestry or ethnicity. Military abductees are no exception. That sort of racism does not happen in The Program. I was *not* picked for this program because I'm Native American. The possibility does exist that I was picked because my father very briefly was tested and used during the origins of the government psychic spying programs years ago. Most likely, from what I've gathered, I was picked up because I've been an abductee since childhood."

In her quest for answers, Jennifer sought help from various investigators and researchers. "I was told by a researcher—a rather zealous one—that there are Program workers who are trained to read auras. When they find individuals who have holes in their aura, it means they have experienced alien contact. These people are tagged to be picked up for The Program. That's one way you get pulled in."

Is there actually a *Program*, as Jennifer calls it? Are aliens really mingling with the military personnel? Or is there something else going on, hidden behind what appears to be an alien-military agenda?

Some abductees, like Charles Fontaine and his wife, have no idea why they were picked. It could be that because of their rural location in Quebec they were easily accessible targets. "Maybe we were just in the wrong place as the wrong time. But for what? What do they want of us?"

Charles' question is echoed by other abductees. And there are no simple answers.

CHAPTER 4
TAKEN

THE ABDUCTION OF A MOTHER AND SON

The night of November 9, 1981 was cold and clear in southern Georgia. The sky was cloudless, strewn with stars, and 38-year old Connie J Cannon was excited.

Connie, an R.N., and her husband and three sons were relocating from their home outside of Atlanta to St. Augustine Beach, Florida. She was driving a brand new Regency Oldsmobile sedan with a V-8, 454-cubic inch engine, a large, powerful automobile that was a dream to drive, especially on I-75. The rear seat and trunk were loaded with boxes of belongings. Her youngest son, John, 12, was in the passenger seat and they were following a huge moving van driven by her husband, Ted, who was accompanied by their other two sons. They were about a hundred miles south of Atlanta, near Macon, with negligible traffic, when suddenly she was no longer on the interstate.

Connie was certain she hadn't taken an exit. Yet, she and her son were now driving on a strange grid of roads with no buildings in sight. She didn't see anything she recognized. She was incredibly tired, but kept driving. The next thing she knew, she and her son were on their knees outside their vehicle, on a black asphalt tarmac near airplane hangars, sobbing hysterically.

Circling overhead were several noisy helicopters and three round, softly grumbling spacecraft. In front of her and John were a group of Grays and several military men in fatigues and heavy boots who held "massive-looking assault weapons."

The Grays seems to be just loitering in the area. But one of the military men pointed an assault weapon directly at Connie, and in a menacing tone warned her, "If you ever…you will never see your family again."

But what was it she wasn't supposed to do or say? Why would the military be concerned about what she might or might not do? Why were aliens mingling with the military? What the hell was going on?

Then she and John were back in the car and she had no memory of actually getting into the vehicle. Where were the military men? The Grays? The choppers and spacecraft? Her son immediately fell into a deep sleep. Connie, barely able to keep her eyes open, recalls driving aimlessly around a labyrinth of paved roads, another asphalt grid, clueless about where she was. No houses. No landmarks. Just another grid of streets. She finally saw a convenience store and stumbled inside. She somehow told the female clerk that she'd gotten lost off of I-75 and could she please give her directions back to the interstate?

The clerk told Connie she was on Warner Robins Air Force Base and had to leave through the same guard gate where she'd entered. Connie explained she hadn't come through a guard gate, but the clerk insisted she couldn't have gotten onto the base any other way. Connie realized that arguing with the woman was futile and besides, she was so exhausted she could hardly speak.

Connie followed the clerk's instructions and eventually found her way back to I-75.

By that time, her husband and other two sons were frantic with worry. When Ted realized that the Olds was no longer behind him, he pulled off the road to wait, thinking they had just dropped back. When they didn't appear after a few minutes, Ted took the next exit and drove northward a while to see if he spotted the Olds by the side of the road. In 1981, there were no cell phones, no way to make contact. He finally figured that Connie and John must have gotten off the interstate for a pit stop or to get a bite to eat, and he and their other sons headed south again.

But Ted stopped once again, pulling to the shoulder to wait for his wife and son. When the Olds didn't appear, the only thing Ted and the other two boys could do was head toward their new home and hope that Connie and John would catch up to them. They arrived at their new house and waited. An hour passed, then another, and Connie and John still didn't show up. Ted, completely panicked, was on the verge of calling the highway patrol when Connie and John finally pulled into the driveway. They'd been missing for three hours.

Connie was too out of it to explain to Ted what had happened. She and John fell into a deep sleep on the porch of their new home and were disoriented for several days afterward. It was worse than jet lag, more like post-traumatic stress syndrome.

"Traumatic doesn't begin to describe the incident," Connie says. "Staring into the barrel of an assault rifle held by one of our own military personnel, while three Grays looked on, was beyond my cognitive abilities."

Warner Robins Air Force Base is located just east of and adjacent to the city of Warner Robins, Georgia, 18 mi SSE of Macon, Georgia. Today, the town of Warner Robins has a population of around 63,000. Macon, the state's fourth largest city, lies a short distance to the north. I-16 intersects with I-75 in Macon and leads to Savannah and the Atlantic Ocean. According to the base's website, Warner Robins AFB "is the worldwide manager for a wide range of aircraft, engines, missiles, software and avionics and accessories components."

Even today, there are long, lonely stretches of I-75 from outside Macon to Valdosta, and at night it's easy to become disoriented. That's especially true if you take one of the rural exits in search for a meal or coffee. Looming to your right and left are thick pockets of darkness your headlights don't penetrate. It's easy to imagine bogeymen out there. You can almost see some alien craft hovering silently, touching down. The imagination is a trickster. Anything seems possible.

Yet, Connie is certain she didn't turn off the interstate. So how did she end up wandering around a "grid of streets" on an Air Force base fifteen to eighteen miles from the interstate? How did she get into the base? The only way to access the base was through guard gates secured by armed military police, and you needed a pass to get in. So how did that heavy Olds, packed with belongings, a woman and a kid, get onto the tarmac? Were they somehow transported by alien technology?

When you step back from Connie's memories, you have to ask what a convenience store is doing on a military base. Yes, there are commissaries. But a commissary is quite different from your local 7/Eleven that sells gas, beer and wine, cigarettes and lottery tickets.

SCREEN MEMORIES AND MISSING TIME

Two of the common elements in alien abduction scenarios are missing time and screen memories. Missing time is what Connie and her son experienced—three hours. A screen memory is something that's implanted in your subconscious, a substitute for what actually happened, a lie. Were the military officers actually Grays, who had shape shifted, a ruse created by the aliens to confuse and distract from what was actually happening? Were

Connie and her son even on a military base?

We met Connie in 2003 after she read Trish's novel, *Black Water*, and wrote a fan letter. The story features a psychic and bookstore owner whose daughter is kidnapped and taken back in time by a sociopathic time traveler. For the next few years, Connie and Trish exchanged emails, then in 2005, Trish had a psychic reading with Connie. Much of what she predicted unfolded. They stayed in touch.

In February 2009, we started a blog on synchronicity and Connie was one of the first who commented. When we posted her abduction story in October 2010, the comments it generated included some from ardent skeptics who thought she was either lying or mentally unstable.

While abductees tend to be as mentally stable as the general population, they are profoundly traumatized by their experiences and often have memory loss and unexplained physical scars—punctures or incision marks in their skin, scrapes or burns.

One of Connie's most unusual encounters, some years after her move to St. Augustine, occurred in the middle of the night, about 3:30. She awakened to find herself standing on a street corner a couple of blocks from her home, wearing her nightgown. She became aware of a rumbling sensation under her feet and knew what it meant.

Three space vehicles were approaching and she knew the ships held beings that would control her, leave her ill, listless, and despairing. She tried to hide—somewhere, anywhere, in the shadows, under trees. She tried to become an ant, a blade of grass. But to no avail.

A single craft separated from the other two and suddenly she was inside that vessel, seated in what looked like a desk chair. A metal strap automatically stretched across her belly, restraining her. She didn't have any idea how she had gotten from the street to the craft.

Connie felt the ship moving and spinning at the same time, and when it abruptly stopped, it quivered like a leaf in the wind. She felt like puking. An entity loomed in front of her, one of the Grays with large black eyes, a negligible nose, a tiny lipless mouth, and sallow gray skin. He spoke in a metallic voice, a monotone, and ordered her to look down.

She did so and a large shield slid open under her seat, revealing a transparent floor, like a glass-bottom boat at Silver Springs, Florida. Something like an infrared light came on and she could see not only a house below the craft, but she could see inside it—the various rooms and furniture, even people sleeping in their beds.

She wasn't afraid; she was enraged. She demanded, "What? What do you want me to see? These people are asleep. It's the middle of the night. What do you want me to see?"

All the while, the Gray entity was right in front of her, staring into her eyes. That made her even more furious.

Then, just like that, it was morning and she was back in bed.

When she sat up, blood poured from her right nostril, the right side of her body felt numb. The room spun when she tried to stand. She thought she might have had a stroke and shouted for her husband. By the time they reached the hospital, Connie couldn't walk. Her husband had to carry her into the emergency room.

She recovered quickly. A CAT scan revealed that her brain wasn't bleeding. There were no blood clots, no aneurysm, no stroke. Nothing unusual was found, except for a small anomalous shadow that appeared on the right side of her nose in a sinus scan. She later believed it was an implant. She went home without saying a word to anyone about her experience. Yet, she knew it had happened. That it was *real*.

Connie describes herself as a "reasonable, rational, moderately intelligent woman who finds a tremendous degree of joy in her life. I don't think I am prone to hysterics or exaggerations. I've been a hands-on caregiver for the terminally ill, and have worked in medical research and in a technical medical teaching capacity. I'm grounded and fact-oriented."

At the same time, she admits that in the aftermath of an encounter with the Grays her challenge is to remain sane and not to live her life in abject terror.

LONG-TERM EFFECTS

Many long-time abductees experience symptoms that include phobias and various health problems that span decades. Diana Fine, mentioned in the introduction, used to suffer from such severe nosebleeds as a child that when she was nine, her parents had her sinuses cauterized. Connie has ended up in the emergency room a number of times for unexplained bleeding. Jennifer White grew up with a lot of 'night fears' and is still uneasy about 'shadows.' She suffers from periodic migraines that lay her up for days.

An abductee we knew years ago was so traumatized by his experience that his life unraveled at the seams. Don Estrella, whose last name ironically means star in Spanish, retained partial memories of an alien abduction that occurred one Halloween while he was wearing a pirate's costume and his companion was dressed as a clown.

When we met him in the mid-1980s, he was essentially lost and homeless. We were intrigued by his colorful background. He had worked as an assistant to author John Keel at the time Keel was delving into the chilling Mothman saga in West Virginia, which later became a book, *Mothman*. Estrella reveled in telling stories related to the giant red-eyed flying beast. He had also worked in a clerical position at the United Nations, where he started a UFO club. He recalled that then-UN secretary-General U Thant sent someone from his office to attend the initial meeting.

Curious about his abduction experience, we persuaded Don to undergo a hypnotic regression with psychiatrist Dr. Bethhold Schwarz, of Vero Beach, Florida. The author of *UFO Dynamics*, Schwarz had interviewed or regressed hundreds of contactees or 'UFO observers,' as he often called them.

In an article for *Medical Times*, Schwarz wrote that these contactees were not psychotic or suffering from hallucinations and they weren't publicity-seekers. "More, on the contrary, fearing ridicule, they are embarrassed to testify to what they saw."

During the session, Estrella recalled the bizarre scene in which he was abducted on a rural north Virginia road while he and his companion were wearing Halloween costumes. They never made it to the Halloween party. The battery in their car had died and the next thing they recalled was being escorted by three small beings to a waiting circular craft. They joined seven or eight other abductees, all standing in line, in an obvious stupor.

Estrella sobbed throughout the regression as he described being taken aboard, placed naked on a table, examined and probed. While those procedures are commonplace descriptions by abductees, Estrella also recalled seeing strange symbols on the interior wall of the craft. While under hypnosis, he drew several of the alien symbols. But he had no idea what they meant.

While Estrella was haunted for more than two decades by his experience and seemed lost because of it, John Mack pointed out that some abductees have experienced physical healings and spiritual transformations as a result of their abductions. Estrella developed some psychic abilities in the aftermath and, as we recall, was happiest sitting in a restaurant with a cup of coffee and a cigarette and giving free readings to waitresses.

In 1991, Diane Fine worked on the waterfront at a California marina and had to climb numerous stairs each day. Her left knee throbbed constantly. Even though she was a military wife at the time, she hadn't had a chance to go to the clinic. One night, she woke and found herself on a familiar surgical table. A big light shone overhead, but she could still see the alien beings. Four of them were gathered at her feet—three small entities and one large Gray. The larger one always seemed to be in charge and this time was no exception. She realized they had operated on her knee, that they could that, so she asked them "Why don't you fix my auto-immune disorder?"

"We can't. It's karmic. This (the knee) is mechanical."

Then Diane lost consciousness. "The next morning I checked my knee. There was a small incision. It healed within two days. My knee has never bothered me again."

Individuals who undergo spiritual transformation as a result of their experiences, Mack said, are more "open to other realities beyond space/time..." And some abductees experience numerous synchronicities or meaningful coincidences that seem to act as guidance, confirmation, and support.

It seems that merely coming into contact with abductees can result in synchronicity. While we were working on Connie's story about her experience on Warner Robins Air Force base, we happened to check Statcounter on our synchronicity blog, which provides all kinds of statistics about who visits it. We were astonished to see that someone from Warner Robins, Georgia, had arrived at our blog by Googling the phrase: *Warner Robins military secrets.* The search had directed the person to one of our earlier blog posts. In the more than three years we've had the blog, we had never noticed a hit from Warner Robins, Georgia. What are the odds that someone dropped by, using those search words, just as we were writing Connie's story?

Karla Turner, like Budd Hopkins, never believed in the benevolence of an abduction experience. Turner held a doctorate in Old English Studies from the University of North Texas and was a college professor for a number of years. But in the late 1980s, she and her husband began to spontaneously recall inexplicable experiences and later, under hypnosis, the details became much clearer. Karla, as well as her husband and son, were lifelong abductees.

She quit teaching to devote herself full-time to writing and speaking at UFO conferences. Her first book, *Into the Fringe,* published by Berkeley in 1992, recounted these discoveries she and her family had made in 1988, about their abduction experiences. In 1994, she published *Taken: Inside the Alien-Human Abduction Agenda,* which provides accounts from eight female abductees from various parts of the world. Her last book, *Masquerade of Angels*, is about the plight of abductees who are subjected to deception, mind control, and massive manipulation.

As a former college professor who was not only smart but had a sense of humor, Karla was popular at UFO conferences. When you watch You Tube videos from some of her talks, she comes across as a credible witness. She's articulate about what she and her family experienced and adamant in her belief that the alien agenda is as far from benevolent to humanity as cancer is to the physical body.

Before she died of breast cancer in 1996, a cancer that advanced so rapidly that many of her supporters believe she was "eliminated," she provided these suggestions for individuals who find themselves living in the sci-fi world where aliens are real:

Educate yourself about the phenomenon. In knowledge lies some control over the situation.

Release fear. Turner believed that negative entities maintain control through fear. Anger, she said, is a better defense than fear.

Abductees should be aware of how they're reacting; they should learn to step out of themselves, and to maintain perspective.

Maintain a good quality of life.

Be realistic about what can and cannot be done.

Stay close to your families.

Confide your experiences to others. "The hell with the results," said Turner. "You don't need the burden of carrying this around."

"If the terrors of the abduction experience made us grow stronger," Turner said, "it was not because the aliens wanted us to have this strength, but because we willed it ourselves."

FALLOUT

The mysterious physical signs and symptoms that abductees report in the aftermaths of their encounters are now well known: scars, rashes, scoop marks, nosebleeds, lesions, and sinus problems supposedly caused from implants that are inserted during the abduction. In fact, these kinds of details are often the first telling evidence that an encounter has occurred.

One morning, artist and illustrator Jennifer White, who recalls several alien abduction scenarios, woke up with a "shoe burn" on the back of her calf. Even though she couldn't recall that anything unusual had happened during the night, she suspected she had been taken.

Thanks to books and movies and TV, even people who know next to nothing about encounters, and don't even believe they are real, are aware of what these physical signs may mean. People like Charles Fontaine. In the immediate aftermath of his encounter, he examined his own body carefully, looking for scoop marks on his calves and the backs of his legs, pinprick marks, scars from injuries he didn't recall. He suggested that his wife should do the same. Neither found any such markings, but that didn't ease their concern that something from out of this world had intruded into their lives.

Whitley Strieber, like many abductees, believes he received an implant at some point during his abductions. Over the years, he has written about the possible purpose of this implant. Physicians have tried to remove it, but he still has it. Connie says she has two implants. One of them is behind the left mastoid bone; the other is high in the upper right sinus. On an MRI, they both appear to be about the size of a bb or slightly larger, with tiny, cilia-type protrusions all over them.

The radiologist who found them and showed the images to Connie decided they were simply anomalous and nothing to be concerned about. He was going to remove them, but she refused to allow it. "I was and am terrified of having them taken out. I don't know what might happen if they are tampered with."

Diane Fine doesn't appear to have any kind of implant, but her many abductions have left her with an immune system that is severely compromised. Most recently, she was diagnosed as "electromagnetically hypersensitive." It's a term for a phenomenon that triggered such severe seizures in Diane that she had to abandon her home until the electrical wiring was fixed.

Could it be that the abductors sometimes botch their effort to add or remove an implant? Connie believes that's what happened to her son, John, when he was 24 and living at home. A little after midnight on September 6, 1993, she and her husband were asleep when she was awakened by a soft knock at the bedroom door. It was John, the same son who was with her during the Warner Robins encounter. He stepped quietly into the bedroom. "Mom," he whispered. "I've got a problem. My throat's bleeding a lot."

It's bad enough when this happens to any parent. But it's worse when you're a medical professional and your mind immediately slams into the absolutely worst case scenario: *What if it's cancer.*

Connie hopped out of bed, grabbed a flashlight, and she and John went downstairs, where his bedroom was. When she looked into his throat, it was bleeding profusely. She asked him, as any mother would, what the hell had happened. He said that when he came awake suddenly, his bedroom "felt uncomfortable, heavy." He said he didn't like it, so he took his blanket and pillow into the living room and laid on the floor and watched TV awhile and fell into a deep sleep. The bleeding in his throat woke him up.

Connie asked if he had eaten anything with a potentially sharp edge that might have nicked his throat. But he'd had nothing to eat or drink since dinner much earlier. The bleeding didn't stop, and she recognized the fact that it wasn't a nosebleed, that his throat was bleeding. She drove him to the ER at the local hospital. Oddly enough, there were no other patients in an ER that was usually very busy. John was taken immediately into a treatment room and Connie waited for him outside. It wasn't long before a female physician hurried out into the waiting room to talk to Connie.

"Your son tells me you're a nurse. I'd like you to look at this. I've never seen anything like it."

Connie followed her back into one of the treatment rooms, where John lay, his eyes dark and wild with apprehension. The physician turned the bright overhead light toward John and shone it into his throat so Connie could see it, and said, "It looks like a scalpel incision or cut. It's deep. I can't imagine how this might have happened."

Connie says that the incision did appear to be a perfectly straight, scalpel-like incision into the tissue of the back of his throat. It was easily seen. The doctor sprayed a local anesthetic into John's throat and told him and Connie that she was going to see if an application of silver nitrate would stop the bleeding.

Silver nitrate seals internal bleeding in situations where sutures are difficult. Usually, a single application is sufficient to stop bleeding, but John's throat required three. When they left ER, John was told that if bleeding recurred during the night, he should go to an ear, nose and throat specialist the next day for sutures.

The next morning, Connie went into John's room with a flashlight to check on his throat. Not only had there been no more bleeding, but there was *no evidence* that any bleeding had ever occurred. Silver nitrate always leaves a gray/black ash in the area where it's used, but there was no sign of the ash, no cut, no scrape, nothing. His throat looked perfectly normal.

So what happened?

"My son is an abductee," Connie said. "He's very sensitive to energies and it's my conviction that on the night his throat bled, he was visited.

Perhaps the visitors attempted to place an implant or perhaps one was removed, and he woke up before the procedure was finished. After we got back home from the ER, I believe *they* returned and destroyed all evidence that anything had happened."

CHAPTER 5
THE FOG

On a warm, humid August evening, we walked into a crowded outdoor bar in Sarasota, Florida. We had spent the day helping our daughter move into the dorm for her second year of college and were ready to kick back and listen to some music.

We looked for an empty table and settled on what was available, a pair of stools on a partially occupied high-top table. We ordered beers as a band played raucous cover tunes from the Sixties and Seventies. We didn't know anyone in the bar and had no plans to meet anyone.

Considering those circumstances, what happened in the next hour seemed highly unlikely. We were about to penetrate a wall of official silence surrounding a secret U.S. Navy base in the Bahamas linked to UFO activity and sometimes referred to as the Underwater Area 51. The man seated across from us with a raspberry martini in hand had just retired from the navy and his last assignment was as commander of AUTEC—The Atlantic Underwater Test and Evaluation Center—on Andros Island.

AUTEC AND UFO HUNTERS

This seemingly random encounter was a striking synchronicity for us. Just four months earlier, we had visited the island with a crew from the History Channel's *UFO Hunters* program. They had interviewed Rob and pilot Bruce Gernon, co-authors of *The Fog*, the story of Bruce's extraordinary experience in the Bermuda Triangle, which began at Andros Island. The producers had hoped to get a tour of the base and an interview with the base commander, but their repeated requests were ignored. The powers-that-be at AUTEC didn't say no; they said nothing.

In spite of the lack of cooperation, the three UFO hunters and their film crew had decided to drive over to the base and asked if we wanted to join them. As we approached the entrance to the secret base, a helicopter appeared and hovered over the front gate. Was it an attempt to intimidate the History Channel crew, and possibly block out any audio with the noise from the chopper? We kept moving forward until a cop car pulled up to the gate and stopped. It didn't go inside; it just blocked the way. At that point, Bill Birnes, the show's lead UFO hunter, decided it was time to back off. Whether or not the activity was directed at our approach, it was a clear sign that we were not welcome.

While AUTEC provides a terse description of its activities on its web site, the public and the media in particular are not embraced. The only way to receive a limited tour of the base is to obtain a sponsor from within AUTEC. As one long-time civilian employee of the base put it: "You don't get very far. You don't see much and you don't learn anything more than what is already public knowledge." Still, it would have been interesting to see Birnes interview the commander of the base for the program. But it didn't happen.

So now 'Commander Richard,' the man at the helm during our April visit, was seated across from us in a noisy bar. It really begged the question: who or what orchestrates this stuff, anyway?

To our amazement, and possibly because he had retired, he was willing to talk about the base—at least to a limited degree. He was interested in hearing about our visit to Andros and the reason for it. If he thought it was funny that the program was about UFOs, he didn't laugh. However, when we mentioned that some purported abductions by alien beings have been linked to military bases, he decided he needed another martini.

We asked him about the contention that AUTEC was the navy's equivalent to Area 51, operated by the Air Force. He didn't smile or frown. His expression gave away nothing at all. He merely shook his head. "AUTEC conducts underwater testing and research. It's about submarines and torpedoes—underwater vessels, not UFOs."

Andros is the largest and least explored among the twenty-six inhabited islands in the Bahamas. It rests on the western edge of a deep-water basin known as Tongue of the Ocean, with depths as great as 6,000 feet. The testing and research that Commander Richard mentioned relates to preparations for undersea warfare by testing submarines and other underwater crafts.

But might the former base commander have actually provided a cryptic answer? Granted, AUTEC might not be interested in UFOs, but they certainly would take an interest in USOs—unidentified submerged objects. Such objects, in fact, have been reported in those deep waters off Andros.

ENCOUNTERS FROM THE DEPTHS

Curt Rowlett was working on a ship as a civil engineer for AUTEC in 1985 when a USO was picked up on radar. "One evening, we pulled out of the dock, and suddenly, out of nowhere, we had a radar contact pop up directly in front of our ship. It appeared to be a land mass where no land mass should exist." Within seconds, the massive object faded and disappeared from radar, suggesting that whatever it was had sunk into the depths.

That sighting could have been a radar glitch. However, it wasn't the first time that Rowlett had seen an enormous underwater object. Five years earlier, while in the Coast Guard, Rowlett had witnessed another inexplicable 'land mass' in the deep waters off Andros Island. "We pulled away from the AUTEC dock well after nightfall, and I was at the helm watch," he recalled. "Suddenly, the officer of the watch told me, 'Hey, I've got a radar contact showing land dead ahead about three miles.' That was patently impossible, because we were in the Tongue of the Ocean and it's a thousand fathoms deep."

The object was "the size of an island," Rowlett said, a blob on the radar measuring between one and two miles in diameter. Meanwhile, the compass needle lashed about wildly. Rowlett didn't know what was happening and wondered if he was in danger.

About three minutes later, when they were about a mile and a half from the 'land mass,' it vanished from radar and the compass stopped spinning. He noted that radar only picks up objects at sea level so whatever it was might have descended out of range. The captain was awakened, and he took the incident seriously, entering it in the ship's log. The radar was tested the next day and found to be in perfect operating condition.

Twelve years earlier, another former AUTEC employee had a similar experience. Dave Malcolm, who was then a weapons technician at the secret base, was working on a torpedo retriever boat in early 1973. It was a typical mission and the vessel had stopped in the testing range about twenty miles from Andros to collect a torpedo. Malcolm stepped out on a platform that extended from the boat just below the surface of the water for easy retrieval of spent weapons. Suddenly, he saw a massive structure rising rapidly directly behind the boat.

Visibility in that water was good, but the day was a little gray and the water a bit rough. "I clearly saw what at first appeared to me to be a pipeline and remember thinking: *What's a pipeline doing in the middle of the water?"* As the object continued rising, he realized it wasn't a pipeline and that it was going to collide with their boat.

Then it stopped just below the surface, but he couldn't tell how wide it was or how far below the surface it extended. It was much thicker than a torpedo and much narrower than a submarine, two objects that were familiar to him in his work. It seemed to hover for a few moments, then slowly retreated, sinking out of sight.

He had no time to call out to anyone, and no one else saw the object. Thinking about his orders, he decided not to say anything about it. "This was during a time when a top secret clearance was taken very seriously and it was hammered into us that we would never discuss what we did or saw. I still have the security manual that describes the term in federal prison for violating the need to know."

Dave had never seen anything like it and had no idea what it was. He thought at the time that it might be a secret experimental craft, but over the years his doubts have grown. Secret crafts, he noted, usually become public knowledge after a time, but in all these years he has not seen or heard of any underwater craft similar to what he witnessed that day.

Considering its cylindrical shape, it's possible to imagine that Dave was looking at the outer edge of a saucer-shaped craft that had risen vertically. In other words, most of the vessel was below the surface, out of sight, and he saw only the rim. Its crew or sensors detected the boat and it retreated into the depths.

INTO THE TRIANGLE

While AUTEC has been compared to Area 51, the secret base is closely linked with the Bermuda Triangle saga. One of the most notable stories from the infamous triangle involves a South Florida pilot who flew out of Andros Island and into the heart of the Bermuda Triangle phenomenon. Unlike many pilots and crews of ships, Bruce Gernon survived his encounter and has been talking about it ever since.

He has appeared on numerous documentaries on the Bermuda Triangle, so many that he's sometimes recognized by strangers. A few months after our trip to Andros for the History Channel, Gernon was eating dinner at the bar in a restaurant when he noticed a man on the opposite side of the horseshoe staring at him. The man whispered something to the bartender, who then came over to Gernon and asked if he was the pilot who had had the strange Bermuda Triangle experience. When Gernon said he was, the bartender told him the gentleman said he worked at AUTEC and would like to talk to him.

There happened to be an open seat next to the man during the crowded dinner hour, so Gernon joined the stranger. The man, who was wearing a t-shirt with an AUTEC logo emblazoned on it, told Gernon that he was still employed at the secret navy base and wasn't going to tell him his name. But for the sake of convenience, let's call him Earl. He said he'd had two unusual experiences during his time working as a civilian employee, but was only willing to tell Gernon one of them.

"So what is it?" Gernon asked.

Earl explained he was working as an engineer on a submarine near the south end of the Tongue of the Ocean when the electronic equipment suddenly acted as if it were possessed. It was as if they had entered a space where the known laws of physics collapsed. Several seconds passed, then everything returned to normal. Everything except that they were now near the north end of the Tongue of the Ocean, about 100 miles from where they had been moments earlier. No one could explain what had happened.

Gernon was fascinated and could only imagine what the second story—the one Earl wouldn't talk about—must involve. Even though the incident took place deep below the surface, Gernon was intrigued by the similarity to his own encounter in the Bermuda Triangle on a flight that began on Andros Island. Gernon, like Earl, experienced an apparent leap in space and time after his electronic equipment malfunctioned.

IN-FLIGHT ABDUCTION

Gernon's story began on the morning of December 4, 1970. It was rainy on Andros, so 24-year-old Gernon, his father, and Chuck LayFayette, a business associate, waited until 3 p.m. for the weather to clear. Gernon took the controls of their new Bonanza A36, and lifted off from Andros Town Airport. The Bonanza was a stable, smooth-flying aircraft, and Bruce was confident of his abilities. They had made similar flights numerous times in search of an island where they hoped to build a resort, and had decided that Andros, with its American military connection, would be ideal.

As he carved a turn, Gernon looked back to the terminal where he saw his friend, John Woolbright, a mathematician at AUTEC, waving to him. John had spent the afternoon with them while they waited for the weather clear, and had stuck around to see them take off.

They climbed to 1,000 feet, but couldn't go any higher because of the cloud-ceiling at 1,500 feet. They tuned into the Bimini radio beacon on their automatic direction finder and headed toward it. They were cruising at 180 miles an hour and had been airborne for ten minutes when the light rain ended and the sky cleared. They had reached the northwest end of Andros and were flying over the ocean shallows of the Great Bahama Bank. Visibility had improved from about three miles to ten miles and the weather appeared calm.

As they started to gain altitude, Gernon noticed a smooth, white, saucer-shaped cloud directly in front of them, about a mile away. He later would refer to it as a lenticular cloud. However, lenticular clouds typically are seen above mountains or at altitudes of 20,000-40,000 feet. They are also stationary. This cloud looked to be about a mile wide and a thousand feet thick, with the top of it reaching 1,500 feet. It would soon shape-shift into a billowing speedster.

Gernon flew over the cloud and filed a flight plan with the Miami Flight Service. They would fly to Bimini, then directly to West Palm Beach. Miami Radio, the call sign for the flight service, reported clear conditions between Andros and the Florida coast, with a few scattered, isolated thunderstorms of moderate intensity in South Florida. Winds were light and variable.

After picking up the weather report, Bruce casually looked back at the cloud and was startled by what he saw. No longer saucer-shaped, it had transmuted into a huge, cumulus-shaped cloud that was moving rapidly. They were ten miles off shore, climbing at a thousand feet per minute, and the cloud seemed to be building up beneath them, rising at the same rate they were ascending.

After several minutes, they were almost a mile high and the cloud was still rising with them. Then, unexpectedly, the cloud engulfed the plane. They felt an updraft, visibility was abruptly reduced to less than a hundred feet. Gernon increased the speed and they finally broke free of the cloud. They continued their ascent, but the mysterious cloud kept pacing them.

"I couldn't get ten yards above the cloud. Within thirty seconds, it closed around us again," Gernon recalled. "Chuck was getting nervous. He had never come this close to a cloud in a small plane. I assured him that we would break free of it at any moment, and leave it behind."

Suddenly, another updraft provided a burst of acceleration that lifted them above the cloud. But once again the cloud caught up to them. The same thing happened several more times. Worried now, they considered turning back to Andros. That's when they broke free at 11,500 feet. Gernon leveled the Bonanza and accelerated to 195 miles per hour as they moved through clear sky.

Later, he figured that the cloud must have been traveling at more than 105 miles an hour, their climbing speed. "When it stopped its horizontal movement, we were finally free of it. I looked back at the cloud and was astonished at what I saw. The cloud was still rapidly building, and was *enormous*. That small lenticular cloud that we had initially flown over had taken on the shape of an immense squall."

Unlike most squalls, which form in a line, this cloud curved in a perfect semi-circle, radiating outward on either side of the Bonanza, but miles away from the plane. Gernon relaxed and continued on toward Bimini. Then, a few minutes later, another squall appeared to be forming in front of them and, like its twin, it was taking on a semi-circular shape, its arms shooting toward the cloud that was pacing them.

Gernon estimated the cloud towered at least 40,000 feet above sea level. He also noticed something else unusual about it. Typically, cumulus clouds have a base one or two thousand feet above the surface. But this one appeared to emanate right out of the ocean. "We couldn't go under the cloud or above it, and attempting to circumvent it would take us considerably off our flight path."

The cloud didn't appear too threatening so after conferring with his father, also a pilot, they decided to fly into it. They were about 45 miles east of Bimini when they penetrated the misty edges of the cloud formation. Once inside, Gernon realized they might have made a mistake. While the cloud was white and fluffy on the outside, its interior was as dark as nightfall. But within seconds, bright white flashes lit up the interior of the cloud. The deeper they penetrated, the more intense the flashes became.

Gernon realized it was too dangerous to continue on their present course and turned 135 degrees so they were heading due south. All three men noted that it was 3:27 PM when they deviated from their course. Upon takeoff, Gernon had engaged an electric-powered clock on the panel that included a timer. It now indicated that they had been airborne for twenty-seven minutes. His father turned on the timer on his watch as they altered their course, and using high frequency OmniRange navigation equipment (VOR), he calculated that they were forty miles southeast of Bimini. Gernon, meanwhile, contacted Miami Radio on the VH and told them that they had altered their course to avoid a thunderstorm and were attempting to fly around it.

They reached clear air again, but within minutes realized they couldn't go around the cloud because its arms were embracing the limbs of the cloud they'd encountered near Andros. As far as they could tell, they were surrounded by enormous rings of clouds, trapped inside a 30-mile wide donut hole.

THE TUNNEL VORTEX

Gernon tried to remain calm as he puzzled over how they'd gotten into this predicament. It almost seemed as if the unusual lenticular cloud they'd skirted near Andros had pursued and trapped them, as if it were consciously directed.

They'd flown about ten miles from the point where they'd turned south when Gernon noticed a U-shaped aperture, a breach in the massive ring of clouds. He figured it was where the two arms of the cloud formation had not yet joined together. At the top, on either side, the clouds extended outward, creating the appearance of two anvils, a shape commonly seen in cumulonimbus thunderstorms. The top typically spreads outward for several miles at an elevation of about 35,000 feet. Normally, Gernon would avoid such cloud formations, but their situation called for drastic action. He turned the Bonanza 90 degrees and headed for the opening, the only way he saw of escaping the cloud.

As they flew toward the aperture, the two anvil heads connected, forming a tunnel, and when they neared it, they realized its diameter was shrinking. Gernon accelerated to maximum power, but by the time they were still three miles away, the tunnel had shrunk to a mere thousand feet across. After another mile, the opening had shrunk to only five hundred feet wide, and as they entered the tunnel it was barely three hundred feet across. But they could see blue sky in the distance.

Once inside the tunnel, Gernon was startled by strange spiraling lines along the entire length of the inside walls. Moments before, the tunnel had appeared to be ten miles long, and he had estimated it would take them three minutes to pass through it. But now the tunnels had shrunk to just a mile in length. Gernon figured it would take them about twenty seconds to pass through it.

"I had to remain right in the center of the tunnel, because I was afraid that if the wings ran into the edges of the cloud, I might lose sight of the hole and the path to the clear sky."

The silky white walls of the tunnel glowed with light from the afternoon sun. The walls shrank and small puffs of gray clouds swirled counterclockwise around the airplane, moving at a rate of several times a minute.

The diameter of the tunnel was now a mere thirty feet and the tips of the plane's wings scraped the edges of the cloud as they reached the far side of the tunnel. The moment they exited the passage, Gernon and his two passengers felt as though they were weightless, that their seatbelts were the only things keeping them from levitating out of their seats. "I felt the strange sensation of zero gravity and also felt that our speed was increasing."

After about ten seconds, the weightlessness vanished. Gernon looked back and gasped; the tunnel collapsed in on itself and formed a slowly rotating slit. He was relieved that they'd made it through, but was acutely disoriented and asked his father to check their position.

His dad was an expert at using the aircraft's state-of-art equipment to find their exact location on the chart. However, this time he fiddled with the instruments for longer than usual. "Then he told me something was wrong. That was when I realized that all the electronic and magnetic navigational instruments were malfunctioning. Even the magnetic compass was slowly rotating counterclockwise, as if the plane were making a turn."

Gernon immediately notified the Miami air-traffic control that he wasn't sure of his position and would like radar identification. The plane was equipped with a transponder, a new invention at the time that helped radar controllers pinpoint the location of airplanes. "I told them we were about 45 miles southeast of Bimini and flying at 10,500 feet. But the controller came back and said that there were no planes on radar between Miami, Bimini, and Andros. That's when Dad snatched the microphone and yelled at the controller.

"What the hell do you mean you can't find us on radar?'"

The controller apologized, but said the radar showed no blips in the area where they were flying. "I wondered how this could be," Gernon recalled. "In the past they had always been able to identify us, especially when we were approaching ADIZ, the international defense zone."

His father was becoming more and more upset and kept screaming at the controller. He and Chuck were starting to panic. Bruce did his best to calm them down, told them they were through the worst of it, that everything would be okay, and struggled to believe it himself.

"Something very bizarre had happened. Instead of the clear blue sky that we expected at the end of the tunnel, everything looked a dull grayish white. Visibility appeared to be more than two miles, but there was absolutely nothing to see—no ocean, no horizon, no sky, only a gray haze."

This stuff was darker than the common haze he often encountered on flights. But the air was stable and there was no lightning or precipitation. "We seemed to be in some sort of fog. But unlike the usual fog where visibility is limited to a few hundred feet, we could see much farther." More disturbing, though, was the fact that the instruments continued to malfunction.

Since Gernon didn't have any idea what might happen next, he cut the plane's speed to 180 miles per hour. The compass kept spinning, it was impossible to tell where the sun was, and he was terrified that they could be moving in any direction, even right back into the mysterious cloud.

At this point, they'd been traveling for nearly thirty-two minutes and should have been approaching the chain of Bimini Islands, which extend fifty-five miles south of Bimini, the main island. Gernon estimated they were about ninety-five miles southeast of Miami.

As they continued on, Gernon felt more confident that his 'internal compass' was keeping them on course and they would soon see the Bimini chain. But the atmosphere remained shrouded by the odd haze and he was mystified by the conditions. "We remained on the Miami frequency, but didn't hear any transmissions for several minutes, which seemed strange. Then, suddenly we heard the voice of the controller, who yelled that he'd spotted an airplane directly over Miami Beach, flying due west."

TIME WARP

Gernon looked at his watch and saw that they had been flying for just under thirty-four minutes. "We couldn't possibly be over Miami Beach yet, so I told the controller that we were approximately ninety miles southwest of Miami, and still looking for the Bimini Islands."

Abruptly, the fog started to break apart, but it didn't just dissipate. Long ribbons of fog ran parallel to their direction of flight, and spread apart until clear sky appeared as long slits in the fog. The ribbons were about one mile from the plane, and extended two-to-three miles in front of the Bonanza, and about the same behind it. The slits gradually grew wider and wider until the ribbons of fog disappeared. "All I could see was brilliant blue sky, and then my eyes adjusted to the brightness, and I recognized Miami Beach directly below us."

The three men were relieved, but completely bewildered. Gernon sensed it was important to remember the details of this flight and the clouds that he'd seen. It was a bizarre thought, almost as if it had come from outside of him. "The clouds were certainly extraordinary, but I had no idea how or why they would be significant."

As they turned and headed up the coast to West Palm Beach, Gernon's father pointed out that the navigation instruments appeared to be working again. After they landed, Gernon thought something was wrong with the plane's timer. "But all our watches showed that it was 3:48 p.m., and the airplane clock showed the same thing. It meant we had made the flight in *forty-seven minutes* and that was clearly impossible."

Gernon had made this flight between Palm Beach and Andros at least a dozen times and had never flown it in less than *seventy-five minutes*, and that was on a direct route. This flight was indirect and had probably covered a distance of close to two hundred and fifty miles. The Bonanza couldn't possibly travel that distance in forty-seven minutes; its maximum cruising speed was 195 miles an hour.

Another year would pass before Gernon heard the term 'Bermuda Triangle' as the legend of missing ships and aircrafts tipped into public awareness. That was when he realized that his experience was part of a larger, much stranger picture.

THE BIG PICTURE

For years, Bruce Gernon puzzled over his experience with the mysterious cloud, the tunnel and the fog, the plane's apparent disappearance from radar, the time distortion.

In 1974, he saw a news program that featured Dr. Manson Valentine, who was leading a group of researchers investigating the Bermuda Triangle. Valentine was the director of the Miami Museum of Science and had astonishing academic credentials—three PhD degrees from Yale in zoology, paleontology and geology. In spite of his academic achievements, he pursued interests that strayed far from mainstream science—interests like the Bermuda Triangle, Atlantis and UFOs. In fact, Valentine's research would play a large role in Charles Berlitz's bestseller *The Bermuda Triangle,* and its sequel.

After watching the program, Gernon called the museum and left a message for Valentine, who contacted him a week later and arranged for a meeting. They met at Valentine's house in downtown Miami, a well-kept older home that belonged to another era of Miami and was virtually surrounded by high-rise buildings.

Valentine was fascinated by Gernon's recollection of his perilous flight from Andros Island. After he'd heard the entire story, Valentine turned to his wife, Anna, and said: "This is amazing. He is the only pilot to have ever flown through the heart of the storm, from its birth through its maturity and to exit through the vortex."

Before Gernon left, Valentine told him that he held the key to the mystery of the Bermuda Triangle. In Valentine's mind, that key related to UFOs. He thought that the elliptical-shaped cloud, which spawned the storm, was hiding a UFO. He went on to suggest that there was a connection between the Bermuda Triangle and Atlantis, and that UFOs were the link. He thought the crafts might be time-travel machines that moved through portals in the Bermuda Triangle between Atlantis and other worlds or dimensions.

When Rob and Gernon wrote *The Fog*, published in 2005, Gernon wanted to avoid linking UFOs to his experience. Like Charles Fontaine of Quebec, he didn't want to be identified as a 'UFO nut.' He also was convinced that the loss of planes and boats in the Bermuda Triangle was related to a mysterious and unknown geo-meteorological phenomenon that he called 'electronic fog.'

The fog, he believes, is created through the release of electromagnetic energy from the earth through the water and atmosphere. Electronic fog can affect compasses and electronic equipment, and even distorts time. It has the ability to attach itself to airplanes or ships, thus creating the deceptive impression that the crafts are moving through a large mass of fog. According to Gernon's theory, such fog typically is no more than a quarter of a mile in diameter.

If electronic fog is related to UFO activity, Gernon didn't want to go there. Yet, in the aftermath of his Bermuda Triangle experience, he seemed plagued by UFO sightings. He has seen UFOs on at least twenty occasions, including a dramatic encounter during a flight just a month after his perilous trip from Andros Island.

It was a perfect night for a flight, calm and clear. His girlfriend had never flown in a small plane at night and decided to join him. It was about 9:00 p.m. when they lifted off from Palm Beach and flew south along the coast. They climbed to 10,000 feet to get a better view of the city lights. When they were directly over the Miami Airport, Gernon turned east over the Atlantic, leaving the lights behind. "When we were a few miles off-shore, the darkness of the sea appeared as a vast black abyss."

Gernon was near the same area where he'd exited the 'tunnel vortex,' as Valentine had called it, when he noticed an orange light to the southeast that was about the size of a planet. It was just above the horizon and appeared to be moving slowly. Suddenly, the orange light grew larger, assumed the shape of a disk, and they watched it in amazement as it moved directly toward them at an incredible speed.

"Within ten seconds it was right in front of us and it was enormous," Gernon recalled. "The disk appeared to be more than a hundred yards wide and thirty yards thick. It was bright amber and filled the entire windshield as it continued toward us. It looked metallic, about three times the size of a Boeing 747. I was sure we would be demolished."

Adrenaline pumped through him, his girlfriend gripped the edges of her seat, braced for impact. Seconds before the craft would hit them, Gernon veered sharply to the left, turning as hard as possible, certain they had no chance of avoiding a collision because they were so close to the object. But, somehow, the huge craft missed them.

He quickly glanced back. There was no sign of the UFO. How the hell could it have disappeared so quickly? Why had it flown directly at them? And why had he climbed to the same altitude and location where he had exited the tunnel vortex a month earlier? Gernon still doesn't have the answers.

One explanation is that possibly more happened than Gernon remembers. Could it be that he and his passenger and the plane itself were abducted by beings that could literally freeze time? What appeared as an instant could have actually involved substantially more time if the abductors were able to capture the craft and shift it into a dimension outside of linear time. Whatever happened, Gernon and his passenger returned to Palm Beach Airport without incident, but were bewildered and uncertain about what had happened.

A few years later, on Dec. 31, 1974, a similar craft appeared while Gernon was in the air, as if to remind him of the previous encounter. This time, however, he was on a commercial flight heading south along the Florida coast. He and his wife, Lynn, and other passengers watched a large amber-colored craft for several minutes.

The plane was descending toward Palm Beach International and was about fifty miles north over the city of Stuart when they first saw the UFO. "We were about 6,000 feet up and three miles inland. It was 7:25 p.m. and I was looking east toward the ocean when a disk-shaped object appeared at an altitude of 3,000 feet. It looked like the UFO that I'd almost collided with four years earlier. It was the same color and it seemed to glow from within, creating a metallic appearance. On the upper portion I noticed a bulge, like a cap, similar to a cockpit."

At first it was moving slower than the plane, which actually passed it. Before it disappeared from sight, he took several photos. They show an object that appears distant and somewhat hazy against the dark sky. Yet, it seems to be an oval-shaped craft with a clearly visible bulge at the top.

The next night Gernon had a strong urge to drive to the beach. He told Lynn that he felt that they would see another UFO. So they headed to Delray Beach, and brought along binoculars with zoom lenses. The weather was clear, the sky cloudless, visibility was more than ten miles. Sure enough, they spotted a UFO and watched it for about ten seconds as it moved swiftly across the sky. Just as it disappeared to the south, another appeared to the north, identical to the first one. It also traveled south at an incredible speed. Then a third one appeared, seemingly following the same flight path. It was followed by a fourth and a fifth disk-shaped object. Zooming in with the binoculars, Gernon could see that they were identical in shape and color to the one he'd seen the previous night.

The last one flew closer to shore, about ten miles out, and traveled at the same high speed as the others. "When it was almost adjacent to us, it made a remarkable maneuver, a high-speed 90-degree turn, with no curvature in its flight path. It headed due west at an altitude of approximately 2,000 feet, and within a few seconds it passed within half a mile of us. When it reached the mainland, it flashed a blue light several times, then vanished."

While he is still wary of being identified as a 'UFO nut,' Gernon has come to believe that UFOs probably play a role in the Bermuda Triangle phenomena, that the area might be an inter-dimensional portal, just as Manson Valentine described it all those years ago.

TARGET OF OPPORTUNITY

In April 2009, we flew in Gernon's Cessna 182 to Andros Island from West Palm Beach for the interviews with the History Channel program. He had last made the flight to Andros three years earlier with a Discovery Channel crew, but they hadn't landed. Now he seemed somewhat nervous.

As we approached the island, the water suddenly glowed with a neon brilliance. It was like seeing a special effect in a movie—the Northern Lights glowing beneath the water. The phenomenon lasted several seconds, we all saw it, but didn't know what to make of it. We figured it was just a reflection of sunlight, yet Gernon thought it was significant.

On our return flight three days later, something unusual happened inside the plane. It wasn't something we saw, but something we *didn't* see.

When we took off, the closest islands—Nassau, the Berry Islands, and Freeport—were visible on the radar screen. Gernon's plane has a state-of-art glass panel, the Garmin G-1000, an avionics device that makes flight information easier to scan and process. You could see the vast reaches of ocean interspersed with named islands.

Gernon flew us over the base for a closer look at the facility. It's technically military air space and potentially dangerous if weapons are being fired. He had flown over the base with the Discovery crew three years earlier without any repercussions. But this time as we passed over the base, the plane's radar screen went blank.

While satellite radar sometimes has temporary glitches and disappears, it's highly unusual for the land masses to vanish completely from the moving map. All 700 islands of the Bahamas were simply gone, 5382 square miles of the Atlantic dotted with lands were suddenly reduced to nothing but ocean.

Bruce didn't say anything, but we were sitting in the back seat and Trish, who had taken flying lessons years earlier, called Rob's attention to it. Fortunately, the weather was clear and Bruce was familiar enough with the route to follow the chain of Berry Islands and use them as visual cues to find his way to Freeport. From there, we headed directly west. The radar screen remained blank the entire trip back.

As soon as we reached the mainland, the screen lit up. Gernon had the radar tested the next morning, and was told that it was functioning perfectly. So what happened?

We clearly violated the airspace restrictions over AUTEC and it's a bit too convenient to attribute the Cessna's loss of radar to some random glitch in a new piece of equipment. When we related this story to former AUTEC employee David Malcolm, he laughed and replied, "They zapped you. You were a target of opportunity."

CHAPTER 6

HIGH STRANGENESS

High strangeness: events or experiences, often associated with UFOs encounters, that are startling and unusual, and involve synchronicity and other psychic phenomena.

STRANGERS WHO KNOW TOO MUCH

In the aftermath of his frightening encounter in rural Quebec, Charles Fontaine desperately searched for answers. In doing so, he encountered an array of enigmatic circumstances, including strangers who knew things they shouldn't know.

On the night following his early morning encounter, Charles woke up repeatedly, fretful and frightened that they were coming back for him, that they would wipe his memory clean. He kept touching the baseball bat that lay at his side, looking around, hoping he was alone in the basement. Finally, the night passed. "I didn't wake up at 6 a.m., I just stood up. I had been awake for a long time."

He remained wary as he headed upstairs, baseball bat in hand. He took a quick look toward the patio door and moved away. "I was still afraid, acting like a coward."

He noticed that Spot remained huddled in the master bedroom. He didn't move or ask to go out. Spot *remembered*.

Even though he was exhausted, Charles got ready for work as usual and arrived on time. He was still deeply confused, depressed, and even haunted by suicidal thoughts. His head throbbed, he felt it constantly, and had trouble focusing on his work. He hid in his office, weeping from time to time.

Unable to focus on his work, he decided to leave the office early. He picked up his daughter at college and drove home. He exchanged small talk with Bridgette, but his thoughts repeatedly returned to the encounter.

Upon arriving home, he walked behind the house and looked for clues or traces of what he had witnessed. He jumped across the ditch to the farmer's field where he searched for traces, evidence of what he'd witnessed, anything disturbed or unusual. His feet crunched over the frozen plowed ground as he plodded through the area where he'd seen the cones of light. But he found nothing other than frozen plowed ground.

Charles looked toward the farm to the south, which was about a thousand feet away, not far, and wondered if the farmer had seen anything. "Every morning after I get out of bed and let the dog out, the farmer is already in his barn. All the lights inside the barn are turned on and by then he's probably already milking the cows."

He walked over to the farmhouse, greeted the farmer, and asked him if he had noticed lights or anything strange in the field yesterday morning around 5 a.m. By the look on the man's face, Charles quickly realized he hadn't seen anything. "What do you mean by lights and something strange?" the farmer asked.

Charles didn't want to tell him the truth and risk being labeled the village idiot who believed flying saucers were visiting him. "I saw some people on ATVs riding on the field near the ditch and thought they could have been thieves at that time of day." He left, disappointed that the farmer hadn't seen anything.

He decided to visit another neighbor, and that was when he would get his first hint of the strange events that would follow.

He knocked on his neighbor's door, and after greeting the man, asked what time he usually got up for work. He said between 5 a.m. and 5:30 a.m.

"Did you see anything strange yesterday morning behind the house in the field?" Charles asked.

The man remarked that he didn't remember if he had looked behind the house. That was when his wife, Erica, called out from the basement. "What? Have you seen a UFO?"

She wasn't laughing. She actually sounded nervous. Again, Charles decided against describing what he'd seen. Instead, he told them the same story about the ATV riders that he told the farmer. But Erica wasn't convinced. "Have you seen a UFO? I know that's it. Tell me, is that what you saw?"

When he hesitated, Erica rushed on: "This is weird, because a couple weeks ago I got a call from one of my cousins. Someone I haven't seen for years, and who has never come here. He claims he's a medium, but we always thought that he was just a weirdo. He became that way after his mother passed away. He said that his Beings of Light told him that we might witness strange lights appearing very soon. He said not to be afraid, that they are good and harmless."

Finally, Charles said that he didn't know exactly what he had seen and asked them not to talk about this in the town. When he got back home, he started telling Helene about his investigation and the incredible comment made by the neighbor's cousin. "But honestly, I was still thinking at that time that none of it could be possible. There had to be an explanation. I didn't want to believe in aliens or Beings of Light—especially not in my backyard! Before March 28, 2011, UFOs didn't exist for me."

Ten minutes later, the phone rang. It was Erica, the neighbor's wife, telling Charles she had just called her cousin, Henri, and told him that the neighbors might have seen UFOs. "Henri says you should not be afraid. His Beings of Lights knew the UFOs were coming. You can call him, Charles, if you like." She gave Charles her cousin's phone number.

Charles stared out the patio door, into the growing dusk. He felt apprehensive, yet figured he had nothing to lose. Why not contact the medium?

But Helene was against it. "You're still in shock. I don't think it would be a good idea. Please be careful," she added when she realized that he was still going to make the call.

Charles wanted to understand what had happened and he was willing to get information any way he could. He made the call. After he told Henri who he was, Henri greeted him and asked how he was doing. Instantly, Charles started crying. He confessed that he was deeply afraid, desperate, and exhausted. Henri told him not to be afraid, that there were good and bad ones. But those that visited his backyard were good.

At some point, Henri sounded as if he'd gone into trance and talked on and on, using spiritual terms Charles didn't understand. He groped desperately for a way to end the conversation. Finally, he interrupted. "Henri, why me?"

After a silence, Henri replied, "Because you are down to earth."

"What happened when I blacked out? Where is that lost time?"

"They didn't want you to see some things."

"But what do they want from me?"

Henri paused again. "Give yourself time. It will all come to you. Give yourself time and be receptive."

When Charles asked if Henri's Beings of Light were the ones in his backyard, Henri said no. Charles was becoming confused. He didn't understand who these Beings of Light were and how they knew about the visitation in his backyard. Henri simply said he wanted to talk to Charles in person, and they agreed to meet in a few days.

After Charles hung up, he thought Helene might've been right. Maybe he shouldn't have called Henri. Was he really a medium? He didn't know. Charles immediately regretted the plan to meet him. In spite of Henri's insistence that the early morning visitors were benevolent, Charles didn't feel any better. Why was he still so afraid if these visitors were benevolent? Maybe Henri didn't know what he was talking about. But how had he known about the UFOs two weeks before the encounter?

ABOUT SPOT

In the coming days, the experience remained on Charles' mind. Both he and Helene were exhausted and their various physical ailments didn't let up. He had constant headaches. Helene complained about the relentless pressure in her head, and her eyes itched all the time. Even Spot wasn't himself. The dog refused to get off the bed, wasn't eating, and hadn't gone outside for two days. At one point, Helene suggested they should sell the house and have the dog euthanized.

Charles knew she was feeling depressed. So was he. The bizarre experience and related incidents were the only things she and Charles had talked about since it had happened. Charles would soon begin to suspect that the UFO encounter was a kind of magnet for experiences best described as 'high strangeness.'

During one of the endless conversations about what had happened, Spot suddenly let out a yelp of pain from the bedroom. They found him standing on the bed, his eyes dull and lifeless. He was afraid to jump off the bed.

Alarmed, Charles picked him up, cradling the dog in his arms. He seemed ill, depressed, and anxious, just like him and Helene. Charles took him outside in the backyard for a bit, then picked him up and carried him back into the house. He gave Spot some food and fresh water, but he barely ate anything.

"I felt deeply responsible for his condition. It was my fault. I'd forced him to go outside that morning."

Charles decided to take Spot for a walk, something the dog had always enjoyed. But they didn't get far before Spot lifted his left paw and started whimpering. He couldn't seem to put pressure on it. So Charles picked him up again and carried him back to the house. Even though it was 6:30 p.m., he called the vet and explained his dog wasn't feeling well. He was told to come right away and Charles arrived at the vet's within half an hour.

The vet immediately noticed that Spot's eyes didn't look healthy and he was continuously whimpering. She asked when he had started acting ill, and if anything in particular happened to him recently. Charles shook his head. "No, nothing in particular."

Except that he saw UFOs in our backyard and might have been abducted by aliens, Charles thought, but couldn't bring himself to say any of it. It was too over the top. Yet, he suspected it was also the truth. The unspeakable truth.

The vet examined Spot's left paw and said there could be a problem underneath or alongside the paw. It could even be caused by a problem with the dog's neck vertebrae. She prescribed a drug to reduce swelling and inflammation.

Back home, Charles put Spot gently into his pet bed in the basement. The phone rang; it was Erica, the neighbor. "Charles, my cousin Henri just called and asked me to give you a message right away. He said it was important and that you would understand. I hope so, because it's odd."

"What is it?"

"He said that his Beings of Light just sent him a message for you. They want you to check your dog's left paw carefully. There's something either underneath his left paw or on the side of the paw. You should also check the dog's neck for a very small cut. It's where they inserted an implant. You might need a flashlight. Look closely. Henri also said you can call him if you want. He's at home."

Charles hung up and hurled the phone on the couch.

"What is it this time?" Helene asked.

As he explained, he found a flashlight and sat down on the floor next to Spot. Charles managed to gently lift the paw with the intention of examining it closely, but he stopped almost immediately. He was shaking, too afraid to continue. How could Henri call precisely at that time and provide that information? How could he possibly know anything about Spot's paw?

He grabbed the phone and called the medium. He felt defensive and angry that his life was being invaded, first by whatever was inside that craft in his backyard, and now by this stranger who knew too much. "Who are you? How could you know about my dog?"

"My Beings of Lights told me about your dog and they wanted me to communicate this to you." He spoke quietly, and sounded like he was going into trance again. But Charles didn't understand much of what he said, and didn't want to listen. The words frightened him, but he memorized some of them so he could look them up later.

After a couple minutes of spiritual utterances, Henri paused and asked a question. "The light that you saw hanging in your backyard…was it a pure bright white light perfectly round?"

"No, it wasn't round at all, but rather like a vertical tube, a machine not from this world and it scared me like nothing has ever scared me before."

Henri continued to insist that the visitors were well intentioned, but Charles doubted it. Why would he feel so frightened if these visitors were so benevolent? And why would they wipe out his memory of the close contact? Henri explained again that they didn't want him to remember some of the details.

Just before hanging up, Henri blurted, "Look at your dog."

Charles glanced at Spot, who was resting on his pet bed. Henri reported that his Beings of Light were telling him that they were right beside Spot and comforting him at that precise moment. "From now on, he will be resting better," Henri assured him.

After the call, Charles started thinking again that Henri was connected with the *bad* ones, and that they were deceiving him. "I even told myself that maybe he opened up the wrong door and let the bad ones in."

Henri's appearance in the scheme of things also triggered a series of synchronicities. He had entered Charles' life through neighbors, a couple he and Helene didn't know very well and didn't see very often. Yet, in the weeks following the UFO encounter, their paths often crossed. It seemed that they were linked in a way that he didn't understand, and neither did they. He would notice them in places where it was unlikely to see them. For example, he would be at a shopping center or in a restaurant 20 miles from home, and there the neighbors would be.

"It was quite unusual, almost impossible, that I would see them so often. Certainly, they weren't following me. They were just as surprised to see me as I was seeing them. One day I was about seventeen miles from home, sitting alone at a coffee shop, and thinking about all that had taken place, trying to understand it and find some solution. I was wondering who could help me.

"As I left the coffee shop, a vehicle arrived and parked next to my car. Even though there were many other spaces available, guess who it was?

The neighbors. One of them said: 'It's so amazing. We live next to each other and rarely see each other. But isn't it strange that everywhere we go now, there you are!'"

ANOTHER STRANGE ENCOUNTER

But it was the encounters with strangers that were most disconcerting. One day after dinner, Charles felt an urge to visit a friend in a nearby town. En route, he stopped at a drug store. He still had the prescription the colon surgeon recommended he take before the test, and decided to get it filled.

While he was waiting for the prescription, he looked for some non-prescription medicine to help relieve the headaches and insomnia both he and his wife were experiencing. Even though ten days had passed since the encounter, they both still felt a constant pressure in their heads and couldn't sleep more than two consecutive hours. It was wearing them both down. They were constantly exhausted.

He told an employee what he was looking for and she suggested Charles talk with the pharmacist. She walked over to him and relayed the request. A few minutes later, the pharmacist approached Charles, and asked how he could help. He was in his mid-50s, a slender man with thinning gray hair and wire-framed glasses. After Charles explained what he wanted, the pharmacist asked if it was for him.

"For both of us, my wife and me."

"Have you thought about marriage counseling?" he asked in a soft-spoken voice.

"No, no. All is well between us. We don't need counseling."

"*You* could use counseling," the pharmacist said.

Taken back, Charles replied, "No, we are not crazy. Counseling won't help."

The pharmacist moved closer and whispered: "Tell me, where did it happen? Inside or outside the house?"

Shock tore through Charles. What is he talking about? Does he know? How can he possibly know?

The pharmacist repeated his question.

"Outside," Charles said. "It happened outside."

The other man leaned closer to Charles again, whispering once more: "You know, the UFO phenomenon is real and many people are aware of their existence."

He removed a piece of paper from his pocket, jotted down someone's first name and a phone number. "Call this person either tonight or tomorrow. Tell him that André said that you should call him. He will help you."

Then he plucked a bottle of Melatonin off the shelf and said, "This will help you and your wife get some sleep."

Charles left the drugstore with his prescription and the Melatonin, plus the slip of paper. He was stunned and no longer in the mood to visit his friend. He got in his car, exhaustion overwhelmed him, and he started crying.

After arriving home, he called the number the pharmacist gave him. No one answered and he didn't leave a message. He started feeling frightened all over again. How could the pharmacist know what happened to him? *And who is this man he wants me to talk to?*

But it wasn't just the weirdness about the pharmacist. Charles felt more receptive now to a hidden reality, a kind of shadow world that lay behind or beneath daily life. He couldn't explain it. And he often sensed a presence nearby, heard eerie sounds that had no visible source, and saw pools of dark shadows that frightened him. It was as if he were haunted in his own home. He wrote in his journal that evening: *I'm very scared. I can't deny it. Something is near me.* He slept in the basement where he felt more secure, where he could keep some lights on.

The next day he went to work as usual, still feeling strong pressure in his head, still physically drained and lethargic. A constant dialogue ran through his mind: *All I'm doing is thinking and thinking. I must be dreaming. This can't be possible. What have I done? Did I allow something bad to come into my life? Again, I'm thinking seriously about suicide. What disturbs me most is that I keep wondering what or who would be waiting for me on the other side.*

Later that morning, he called Jules, the man the pharmacist recommended. He closed the door to his office when Jules answered. "André gave me your phone number and said you will help me. Has he or anyone called to tell you that I was going to call?"

"I haven't heard from André."

Charles didn't know where to begin. He immediately started feeling emotional. "My voice was shaking, I had a problem making sense, I felt like crying. Before I explained to Jules what it was all about, he told me to take a deep breath and relax. He apparently sensed my distress."

"I know what you saw," Jules said. "UFOs. You have to be aware that you aren't the first and you won't be the last. It happens every day. I won't let you down, but you're in shock.'"

Charles proceeded to describe what had happened to him and Helene and the events in the aftermath. But after a couple of minutes, Jules interrupted him. He said that he was on his way to the lab where he worked as a microbiologist, and didn't have much time to talk.

Charles said he understood and asked Jules what he thought about the medium, Henri. "Mediums are very sensitive people. He is really in communication with those Beings of Light, and he is probably *not* a dangerous person. But considering your condition, you should stop talking to him." Then, rather cryptically, he added, "Faith is your only weapon. You know what you must do. Clean up the house and tell them that they are not welcome. They have to leave."

Charles was baffled by how André and Jules knew what they knew about him. He hadn't mentioned UFOs to either one of them. It was as if they only looked at him or listened to the tenor of his voice, and they somehow knew he'd had an encounter. Combined with the medium's comments and the neighbor woman's knowledge of what he had seen, Charles felt as if he were falling down the rabbit hole, that his world had been turned inside out. He didn't know what to do.

Then he seized on something the microbiologist had said. He would use faith as a weapon.

HOLY WATER

Five minutes later, Charles called the priest in his hometown parish. Without identifying himself, he asked if he could stop by later for some holy water. The priest chuckled. "If you want holy water, all that you have to do is to come to mass next Sunday."

After work, Charles told Helene about Jules, what he said about Henri, and what he thought they should do. The phone rang, interrupting him before he told her about his brief conversation with the priest. Helene answered and after a moment handed the phone to him. "It's Erica, the neighbor," she whispered.

"Henri just called me a few minutes ago. He wants to know if tomorrow is still good for you for his visit."

"Erica, tell him to stay away, that I don't want to see him. Tell him I think he opened up the wrong door. He thinks he's connected with the good ones, but they're lying to him. So they must be the bad ones."

She sounded nervous as she suggested that he call Henri himself. But Charles told her didn't want any further contact with the medium.

"I know what you mean," Erica confided. "It *is* kind of strange. I don't like getting his phone calls and having to call you." After a moment, she added. "I just hope you're not mad at us. You're good neighbors. What have you seen exactly?"

"I saw something that I wish did not exist."

Later in the evening, Jules called. Charles told him about his phone call with the priest about holy water. "I'm mad at the priest. He just left me hanging, telling me that if I want holy water, I should go to mass next Sunday. Then he hung up on me."

"You don't need holy water to clean up the house," Jules said. "Your faith is good enough to kick them out. You're strong enough. Go to every corner of your land and mark your property. In your mind, erect a shield around your property."

They talked for half an hour and afterwards Charles felt better knowing that a pharmacist and a microbiologist didn't think he was crazy. However, by the end of the week, he still felt like he was losing his mind and conceded that his faith wasn't strong enough to get rid of the presence in the house. It seemed to shadow him wherever he went. He didn't know if this presence was invisible aliens, ghosts or spirits. But in his journal, he wrote: *I'm so afraid of mirrors now.*

There's something archetypal about mirrors, something about them that speaks to a deeper part of ourselves. The ancient Greeks used reflections in still water as a tool for contacting ancestors at the Oracle of the Dead. Psychiatrist and author Raymond Moody revived the practice of 'mirror-gazing' when he created a *psychomanteum*, a mirrored room where his patients would seek contact with deceased loved ones.

Mirrors play a similar role in numerous fantasy tales. Alice went through one and emerged in a topsy-turvy world. The wicked queen in *Snow White and the Seven Dwarves* kept asking her mirror who the most beautiful woman in all the kingdom was and when the mirror's image replied that it was Snow White, the queen went ballistic and plotted to kill her. In *Beauty and the Beast,* a mirror enabled Beauty to "see" how her family was doing while she was held captive in the beast's castle; it was a venue for far-seeing, for clairvoyance. For many young children, a mirror is a like a closet, a scary place where another reality exists. And that's how mirrors were for Charles.

I feel like another dimension is in there. I feel like something is going to come out. His fear had become atavistic, instinctive, so deeply rooted in who he was that he was like a little kid cowering in the dark, the blankets pulled over his head.

He finally decided to go to church, but not in his hometown. He drove to a nearby city, and brought along an empty plastic bottle that he'd tucked away in his jacket. After mass, he asked an old woman who helped with the ceremony if he could have some holy water. She was very kind, he recalled, and when he removed the bottle from his jacket, she told him to take as much as he wanted. "It's free and you may come any time you want more."

Arriving home, Charles found Helene stretched out on the couch with a cold compress of towels on her forehead. She complained of a headache and the constant, pounding pressure in her skull, the same sensation that Charles felt. He went immediately to the basement and poured a bit of holy water in his hand, touched his forehead, then took a few sips.

As a Catholic, the holy water held profound significance for him. It had been blessed, it conferred protection, its symbolism was powerful.

Spot was nearby so he poured more in his hand and let the dog lick it. He dipped his fingers into the holy water, touched his forehead again, then snapped his wrist, flicking drops of holy water around the room. "Get out of here. Leave us alone. You are not welcome here. We want to live in peace...in peace with Jesus Christ, our only lord."

He went upstairs and did the same thing in every room. Then he poured some holy water in Helene's hand and told her to rub her forehead. She drank some, too. He walked outside to every corner of the property and even to the sheds. He blessed the land, creating a protective shield around it. His faith sustained him, infused him, empowered him.

Later that same day, he and his wife started feeling better. The headaches abated, the relentless pressure in their heads let up. After that, the couple and their daughter began carrying vials of holy water with them everywhere they went.

MORE SYNCHRONICITY

One afternoon, André and Jules visited Charles and Helene and talked about their encounter. Jules mentioned that most of the people he knows who have encountered UFO phenomena refuse to talk openly about their experiences. Like the Fontaines, they don't want to be ridiculed.

Jules suggested that from now on, Charles shouldn't look at any strange lights hanging in the sky. He advised leaving some lights on inside their house at night. The idea is that abductees might be captured or paralyzed by the use of light rays, similar to how a deer might freeze in a headlight at night. Jules said that if they ever returned, Charles and Helene should turn on the radio, the TV, crank up the volumes, and call the fire department and the cops. In other words, make a lot of noise, create a ruckus. The more people who witnessed the existence of these *entities*, the better it would be for everyone. He also said that *they* could read minds, so he and Helene should tell these entities to leave them alone and go bother someone else.

Aliens, be gone! Other abductees have tried this, of course, with mixed results. In *Communion,* Whitley Strieber writes in excruciating detail about his attempts to drive the visitors away from him, from his wife and son. Bright lights. A gun. Connie Cannon screamed at her abductors, *What do you want from me?* Diane Fine sought relief and answers in Buddhism— mantras, meditation, some higher, broader purpose and reason.

In many ways, an encounter bears eerie parallels to Elisabeth Kubler-Ross' model for the five stages of grief when confronted with impending death:

Denial (this can't be happening to me)

Anger (why me?!)

Bargaining (I'll do this for you if you do this for me)

Depression (I can't go on)

Acceptance (It's going to be ok)

At some point during their conversation, Charles asked André how he knew that Charles had encountered a UFO. He replied that he had an experience himself, an enormous black, soundless helicopter that hovered above his vehicle. It looked like a helicopter, but it wasn't one. He added, rather cryptically, that his brother in-law, Jules, has taught him many things related to UFOs.

Charles considered his contact with these two men as synchronicity. He was looking for help and found it through a pharmacist without asking for anything but over-the-counter sleeping pills. "They came into my life at the right time."

Helene also experienced synchronicities in the aftermath of the UFO encounter, which seemed particularly significant because she, unlike Charles, just wanted to forget about what happened. Her perspective was that something very special happened, they should feel fortunate because few people experience what they did. Beyond that, she didn't want to think about it any longer. She had no interest in getting hypnotically regressed or even reading about UFOs.

One day at work, a client, a man she had known for years, walked into her office and within the first minute asked her if she believed in UFOs. She motioned for him to speak more softly and said that she did. He asked her if she had ever seen them and before she answered he said that he'd had two sightings years ago. In nearly thirty years at the same job no one had ever mentioned UFOs, much less asked her if she'd seen them.

In August of 2012, it happened again. She had taken her car to a garage for servicing and was paying the bill to the service attendant at the front desk when he began talking about politics. He referred to an older man who sometimes came to the garage just to talk politics with him. He said the man was quite interesting and could talk for hours about politics. He said the man even believed that aliens in UFOs were controlling the planet, and that world leaders were hiding the truth because otherwise there would be great chaos.

"This makes sense to you, doesn't it?" the service attendant asked.

Startled by his question, Helene paid the bill and left.

WHEN NEGATIVE IS POSITIVE

One month after Charles discovered that his pants were filled with blood, he received the results of his colonoscopy: negative. The doctor assured Charles he had checked carefully, he knew about the incident with the blood. The doctor was puzzled, didn't know exactly what could have caused it. But he told Charles not to worry. All appeared to be fine. "See you in five years for your next test."

But what caused that spillage of blood? Did it have anything to do with the strange experience in the cemetery? Is there a connection between aliens and the dead?

Perhaps what happened in the cemetery and what occurred in his backyard were unrelated. Yet, in the aftermath of an alien encounter, Charles felt an invisible presence in his house and feared another encounter. At the very least, an odd synchronicity connected aliens and the dead. Some abductees have reported being subjected to painful rectal probes after being taken aboard alien crafts. But Charles linked the bleeding to his experience in the cemetery, the home of the dead.

INTO THE VIAL

After Charles contacted us and related his story, he said that he was look-ing for any way possible to find out what happened to him and his wife that morning. He had gone to a hypnotherapist for a regression, but the session hadn't gone well. She'd tried to take him back to the encounter, but used the wrong day and time. Noises inside and outside her office had also disturbed him.

"At least, I was able to close my eyes and get some rest for awhile," Charles recalled. "I felt more secure. I had someone guarding me while my eyes were closed."

By this time, he and his wife and daughter had been carrying vials of holy water for nearly a year. We asked Charles if he would send us his vial, the one he'd been carrying for months. Our idea was to have it 'psychically analyzed' by a psychometrist –a psychic or medium who works with personal objects belonging to clients.

Kathy Adams lives in Cassadaga, a Spiritualist community in central Florida. We'd had readings with her before and were impressed with the information she had provided by simply holding a ring or other personal object. But what would she pick up from holy water? We told Charles that she might be able to come up with something of interest about aliens or spirits, or both.

He mailed the vial, sealed in plastic, and neither of us touched the glass container, just the upper edges of the plastic around it. Not long after the vial arrived, we drove to Cassadaga, located about 30 miles north of Disney World.

Cassadaga doesn't look like other parts of Florida. It's set within rolling hills covered in pines and oaks, many of the town's buildings and homes are wooden and nearly a century old. The main road through town features a Mediterranean-style hotel built in the 1920s, a New Age bookshop, the post office, and several blocks of houses with signs out front that read, *Medium* or *Psychic* or *Reverend So and So*. Outside the Spiritualist camp are more houses occupied by practicing psychics or mediums, not associated with the camp. No matter where you walk in Cassadaga, there's a mysterious hush in the air that is almost palpable and makes it impossible to forget that you're in a place where nearly everyone communicates with the dead.

On weekends, the town bustles with tourists who have come here for psychic readings. Cars are parked along the sides of the main road, the parking lot of the Cassadaga Hotel is jammed, visitors browse the bookstore and gift shops, walk through the camp and sit on the wide hotel porch, having a bite to eat or getting readings.

That weekend was no exception. We finally found a parking spot near the bookstore and debated about which of us would take the holy water vial to Kathy Adams. Rob thought it was best if Trish got the reading, because a couple of months earlier when Rob had a reading with Kathy, she had picked up on Charles—'a man living in Canada who wants your help.' So while Trish headed to Kathy's place, Rob took our two dogs on a bike ride around Spirit Lake.

Kathy, whose home and work place is located across the street from the hotel, is often heavily booked, especially on weekends. So Trish was surprised that no one was waiting and she got in right away. She sat in Kathy's office, a small room with a desk, computer, and a couple of chairs.

With any psychic reading, we try not to provide any leading information about ourselves. Even though we'd had readings with Kathy before, she sees dozens of clients a week and it wasn't likely that she remembered Trish.

After exchanging pleasantries, Trish brought out her notepad and pen and the vial, still sealed in the plastic wrapping.

"It belongs to someone else," she said, handing it to Kathy. No one else has touched it since he mailed it. You can take it out."

Kathy, an attractive woman in her late forties or early fifties, has a quick, winning smile and eyes that dance with curiosity. She emanates a kind of presence that says she is comfortable in her own skin. Yet, when she took the vial, her expression noticeably changed, and Trish didn't understand why until later.

Sitting in her office chair, she tucked one foot up underneath her thigh, held the tiny vial between her thumb and forefinger and closed her eyes. Trish suddenly realized she had inadvertently revealed that the owner of the vial was male.

Kathy's fingers moved over the glass. "Is this gentleman in a northern city? I see a lot of snow around him."

"Yes, in Canada."

"There's a lotta stuff going on around him...not necessarily spiritual stuff, but...*abnormal occurrences.*"

Trish nearly laughed. *Abnormal?* You bet.

"He's having a difficult time knowing what's real and what isn't. His significant other is going against what he wants to do. She just wants to forget what happened."

Uh, yes.

Kathy paused and rubbed her fingers over the vial again. "A gentleman who lives far away from him is trying to help, and this gentleman— the Canadian—is telling him more and more. You know both of these men."

If the man she was referring to was Rob, then yes and no. Rob had been communicating with Charles for weeks, but Trish knew Charles only through emails and their Skype conversations, as related by Rob.

"Someone who passed away, a relative, has been trying to communicate with this gentleman," Kathy continued.

This reference might relate to Charles' eerie experience in the cemetery he and his father visited shortly before Charles' UFO encounter. His uncle, who had died a few weeks earlier and was buried there, had been estranged from Charles' side of the family.

"This gentleman has other spirits around him now who aren't related to him, a different set of guides, who are trying to help him place things in perspective."

She went on like this for a few minutes, talking about the spirits around Charles. Then Trish offered some history. "The vial belongs to a French Canadian guy who had a UFO encounter and was so freaked out that he started carrying that holy water to protect himself."

"Wow," Kathy said with soft laugh. "When you first handed me this vial, I thought it was filled with urine."

"Really? Why?"

"I handle a lot of urine vials in my part-time work as an ER nurse. I never expected holy water."

"Does the holy water tell you anything about the encounter?"

"They won't be back. This was a one-time deal."

"So he was abducted?"

"Definitely."

"But for what purpose?"

She thought a moment, rubbed her fingers over the vial again. "Entertainment."

Trish thought about that. *Entertainment?* They blow open some random guy's head for *fun*? It's not the typical MO of alien abduction sagas, which often seem to be related to the gathering of genetic material.

However, Brad Steiger, author of numerous New Age books, writes in *UFO Odyssey* that entities occasionally seem to do what they do for fun "....or simply to astonish and disturb the gullible 'for the devil of it.'" It may sound offensive to experiencers who have endured decades of abductions, but what do we actually know about what these beings think and why they do what they do?

Kathy handed the vial back to Trish. "I feel bad for the gentleman. His life burst open because of this. And now he's investigating, researching, digging around for answers. And his significant other just wants to forget it and move on and maybe get their house exorcised."

Although Kathy initially didn't know the details of the *abnormal occurrences* Charles had experienced, her description of his mindset and that he was haunted by something inside his house was accurate. When we told Charles about the reading, he said he hoped she was right that his encounter would be a one-time experience.

That was also when he told us he no longer felt that any entities were following him at home. The house was clean. A synchronicity, we thought. We'd taken the vial of holy water to a spiritualist community, the spirits had been read, and the spirits had fled.

CHAPTER 7
FOSTERING HYBRIDS

Hollywood loves aliens. And with a few exceptions like *ET*, *The Man Who Fell to Earth*, *Abyss*, *K-Pax*, and *Avatar*, the aliens are invariably bad and look utterly hideous. Even though the alien in *ET* isn't exactly a physical specimen of beauty, you love him anyway. You know he's a good guy.

The other attribute that Hollywood's aliens possess is *power*. This power manifests itself in various ways—telekinesis (think Carrie on steroids), telepathy (they read/invade your mind), camouflage (shape shifters), and their advanced technology. The technology usually involves sophisticated weapons that can reduce a city like Manhattan to smoking rubble in just seconds or technology that tears open the fabric of space/time, so that more alien spacecraft can pour into our reality.

In Michael Crichton's *Sphere,* a huge vessel at least 300 years old rests on the ocean floor in the middle of the South Pacific. Its alien crew can manipulate reality itself. What you see, taste, touch, hear, and sense intuitively is completely phony, a camouflage, an illusion, just like the world in *The Matrix*.

All of these stories can be boiled down to a single burning question: *what is the nature of reality*? For an abductee, that answer lies in an area so gray, so muddled, so riddled with inconsistencies that connecting the dots is impossible. Just ask Diane Fine.

MISSING PREGNANCY

In high school, Diane was diagnosed with cystic ovary disease. Ovarian cysts are small fluid-filled sacs that develop in a woman's ovaries. Most are benign, but certain types of ovarian cysts may cause infertility. Diane had three surgeries by the time she was in her late teens and was told she could never get pregnant.

While living in a college town in upstate New York, Diane went to her family doctor because she was feeling so exhausted and frequently nauseous. After a urine test and a pelvic exam, he informed her she was eight weeks pregnant. She was shocked—and so was her doctor. Due to her previous surgeries, he deemed her pregnancy to be high risk and referred her to a clinic in Burlington, Vermont. In that part of New York in 1979, there were no major medical facilities and people had to travel to Syracuse, New York or to Burlington, Vermont, to see specialists.

The trip to Vermont took three hours by car and included a ferry ride across Lake Champlain. The day of her appointment, Diane and her two roommates left early that morning and hoped to explore Burlington for a few hours before her late afternoon date at the clinic. "It was a gorgeous spring day," she recalled. "And our drive was going as planned. We passed Dannemora prison and went through the small town of Dannemora without incident. It's after this that things got very, very strange. "

Just for a frame of reference, the village of Dannemora is part of the town of Saranac in the Adirondacks. It has been inhabited, in one form or another, since 1838, with the town's actual incorporation occurring in 1901. The prison Diane refers to opened in 1845, and was once known as the Clinton Correctional Facility. It was a maximum security facility and employed convicts to work in the iron industry. From 1900 to 1972, Dannemora also housed a hospital for the criminally insane.

Think about that. Seventy-two years of dark energy that infused a particular location, energized it, perhaps even defined it. A place haunted by inmates who had lost their minds in prison and now faced an even worse sentence, as patients in a hospital for the criminally insane. At some point in this period, electroshock treatments were common. Dennamora—the town and the prison—became synonymous among many in New York for the place where the criminal nutcases were confined. It was the kind of place that Ken Kesey described eloquently in *One Flew Over the Cuckoo's Nest*.

Just after passing through Dennamora, Diane and her roommates encountered a thick bank of fog and visibility shrank to practically zero. If you've ever been caught in dense fog, then you know how eerie it can be—vague shapes around you, visibility of less than a foot, that strange dampness in the air, the odor of wetness and earth. It's creepy.

Diane and her roommates saw a gravel driveway just off to their right, pulled in and found themselves outside a big old barn that had been remade into a bar/restaurant. They went inside to wait out the fog, approached the counter, sat down. Diane recalls that the couple behind the counter were older, white-haired. "They were quite short, five-feet tall at the most. They seemed warm and friendly, though I can't remember anything they said."

Diane and her roommates ordered sodas. As they waited for their drinks, she looked around the high ceilinged room and noticed many old photos and farm-related antiques on the wall. She couldn't see anything outside the windows; the fog hugged the old barn. When their sodas arrived, Diane sipped at hers and noticed it was strangely sweet, thick, and warm as it went down. "I had never tasted anything like it before. I have no memory after this point, until two hours later."

The next thing Diane knew, she and her roommates were at the ferry station, preparing to cross to Burlington, with no idea how they'd gotten there. It didn't just feel like the *Twilight Zone*; it *was* the twilight zone. And how had it gotten to be so late in the afternoon? But there was no time to worry or fret about any of it, no time to pick it apart. Diane didn't want to be late for her clinic appointment.

They arrived at the clinic just in time for her appointment. She was called into the examining room, where the nurse practitioner read the doctor's referral. "I see you're eight weeks pregnant," she said to Diane. "Let's take a look."

The nurse practitioner performed a pelvic exam and immediately seemed confused. She called another woman into the room, who looked at Diane's file and also examined her. The women conferred for a moment, then the nurse practitioner announced, 'This is an un-pregnant womb.'"

Diane was floored. "Was the referring doctor mistaken?" she asked.

The nurse practitioner shook her head. "No. Your urine test was positive. He examined you thoroughly. His diagnosis couldn't be wrong. But you are *not* pregnant."

At this point, Diane panicked. "I knew that what had happened in the fog, with the missing time, had something to do with the fact that I was no longer pregnant. But what? This was before UFO abductions were a part of pop culture, so I had no idea what had happened. I didn't mention the fog incident, but I was so distraught the clinic gave me a Valium, then sent me on my way. They didn't have a clue what to say to me."

When Diane left the clinic, she told her roommates she wasn't pregnant. They were as perplexed as she was. They headed home, taking the same route. Before reaching Dennamorra, they looked for the converted barn. "We found the gravel drive, but it didn't lead anywhere. The building *wasn't there.* It was just *gone,* like it had never existed."

Diane and her roommates never discussed the incident again. Not only was it too weird to talk about, but she was deeply traumatized by what had happened. It wasn't until five years later that she read stories of missing time, missing babies, and aliens. "That's when I knew for sure what had happened in that fog, in that barn bar. My baby was somehow *removed* from my uterus during that missing time."

An event that mainstream science considers impossible occurred near a prison whose name is synonymous with insanity. Diane recognized the synchronicity. "It's a dark trickster," she said. "And with these experiences, there are invariably weird coincidences."

THE BREEDING PROGRAM

Diane's experience is by no means unique. In *Secret Life—Firsthand Documented Accounts of UFO Abductions*, Professor David Jacobs of Temple University conducted interviews with more than sixty abductees. Under hypnosis, many of them describe astonishing details about what Jacobs concludes is an alien breeding program.

Jacobs delineates the three stages of gynecological procedures the aliens perform: the culling of ova (which Betty Hill recalled under hypnosis), embryo implantation, which is later followed by embryo and fetal extraction. The second and third procedures are what Diane believes happened to her. "The abductee…may have morning sickness and she may have a 'pregnant feeling,' Jacobs wrote. "She may take a home pregnancy test that shows positive and then she may go to a physician for a blood test that confirms her suspicions—she is pregnant."

Jacobs notes that variables exist in the scenario he described, but that typically, six to twelve weeks into the pregnancy, the woman discovers that she's not pregnant. "She has no miscarriage, no expulsion of fetal material, no indication that something was wrong. She goes to her physician, who confirms that the fetus has suddenly disappeared."

Diane has never recalled any details of what happened during those two hours of missing time. But intuitively, she knows that her baby was taken.

Imagine how such an experience would impact your life, worldview and spiritual beliefs, particularly in an era like the late 1970s when there was practically no information available on this phenomenon. In 1979, books by Hopkins and Strieber, David Jacob, John Mack, Kara Turner and others lay ahead in the future. None of the technologies existed that we now take for granted—no Internet, social media, Google, Smart phones. Stories about abductions, aliens, and UFOs were really fringe stuff. In whom could you possibly confide without being labeled a nut? A wacko?

Today, there are numerous websites and forums where an encounter can be reported and experiences can be explored without fear of ridicule. Yes, skeptics and debunkers still abound. But people like Charles and Helene are far more fortunate than Diane was back in 1979 or Connie was in 1981 in that resources are available to them.

Yet, Diane had an inner resource that helped her through her trauma with this missing pregnancy—and with her other abductions and encounters. When she was barely two years old, she had a significant experience she recalls that gave her the big picture. "The Naga beings, part serpent, part human, visited me, and explained that my current life was going to be very difficult."

She grew up in the St. Lawrence River Valley, near the American-Canadian border in upstate New York. Her childhood was isolated, often violent, and she spent much of her time alone with nature, the woods, and the river. After a particularly severe incident of abuse at the hands of her father, she awakened in the arms of an immensley muscular being. "He was cradling me as he, and others like him, glided through the fields toward the woods behind my home. I felt safe cradled against him and dozed off. When I awakened again, I was in a luminously glowing room that seemed to be in a cave, underground. That's when I saw that the beings I was with were half serpent, half human. They were tending to my battered and bruised body."

The being who told her that her current life would be difficult also said that she didn't have to repeat the behavior that she witnessed. "I knew he meant for me not to hurt others the way I was being hurt. I also knew that my current life was an assignment I had to complete.I felt precious in the presence of these beings, as though I were a jewel. I didn't feel that way among my birth family."

The next morning, when she woke up, she tried to explain to her mother that the dinosaur people had visited her. It was the only term her child mind could come up with to describe what she had seen. She told her beloved grandmother the story as well. Both of them thought she had a vivid imagination.

Diane never saw these beings again, but didn't forget what they had told her. She felt them near her often. "It wasn't until I was thirty-five that

I finally found a name for what these beings were: Nagas and Naginis."

The word *Naga* comes from the Sanskrit. In most languages of India, *nag* is the word for *snake*, particularly the cobra. It's a term used for invisible beings that are associated with water and energy that is fluid. Following her discovery of the identity of her dinosaur people, she experienced numerous synchronicities related to nagas.

We pointed out that one of the favorite arguments skeptics invoke about abduction scenarios is that they mask childhood physical and sexual abuse, which the individual has suppressed. Diane is acutely aware of the argument. But she points out that none of her memories were ever suppressed. "I remember what happened to me. I have always remembered how I was sexually abused. My body remembers."

What she learned from her encounter with the nagas is a testament of the human spirit's ability to rise above its circumstances. "This encounter taught me that I was loved (if not by my parents); that we humans are more than what we appear to be; that there is an eternal aspect to creation; our bodies and lives are one small piece in a very large puzzle; and that the universe is mysterious and magical."

ALIEN HYBRID NURSERIES

As John Mack noted in *Abduction*, the most common procedure to which abductees are subjected involves the reproductive system. "Abductees experience being impregnated by the alien beings and later having an alien-human or human-human pregnancy removed. They see the little fetuses being put into containers on the ship, and during subsequent abductions may see incubators where the hybrid babies are being raised..."

Sound too bizarre to be true?

In 1991, twelve years after Diane's missing time experience, she was abducted again and taken to a nursery on an alien craft, where she was shown a sad, sick little baby. "She needed love so badly. It broke my heart. The Grays don't seem very loving. This is when they actually indicated that they had some of my own children. Is that a harvest or a kidnapping?"

Her intuitive sense that the baby she was shown was actually hers was confirmed several years later, when she stayed at Harmony Grove, a Spiritualist community north of San Diego. She spent an afternoon with one of the mediums who lived there. Diane didn't tell the medium anything about herself. But during the reading, the medium paused and said in a soft, sad voice, "I see they've got some of your babies." Diane notes that the medium never said *Grays or aliens*, but she knew what the woman was talking about.

When Connie Cannon was younger, still of childbearing age, one of her abduction experiences involved the nursery. A Gray placed an infant in Connie's arms and told her the child was hers, that she needed to hold it, *talk* to it, *nurture* it. Telepathically, the Gray told Connie that if she didn't hold the infant, it would die.

"I cried and cried as I held the ugly, deformed little thing."

The experience occurred a few years after the birth of Connie's youngest son. "My tubes were tied in the delivery room after he was born because my insides were such a mess that my OB said absolutely no more children. This ET/hybrid/ baby occurred *after* my tubes had been tied. It wasn't a dream. It was a very real encounter."

Connie said the infant resembled a baby afflicted with progeria—a rare condition in children in which they age prematurely. Such children are typically bald and short, have a wrinkled face and no eyebrows or eyelashes, a large head, dry, thin skin. Think Smeagol, but with a stunted human body and a really *old* human face.

During correspondence with David Jacobs, Connie mentioned the physical similarities between baby hybrids and Progeria patients. Jacobs replied that her observation was interesting, but that there were distinct differences. He didn't elaborate. Yet, Connie continues to wonder whether the children around the planet who are born with Progeria might be hybrid insemination gone awry. "No one can talk me out of that possibility, that idea."

In his book, *Secret Life,* Jacobs provides quite a bit of detail about what abductees experience during a child-presentation. The aliens encourage the abductee to hold the infant, love it, talk to it, even nurse it. A woman who doesn't have breast milk "may be surprised to find that she is lactating and that her breasts are engorged."

When you think about that, when you think about any of it, really, your first urge might be to roll your eyes or politely stifle your laughter. But when these types of experiences and impressions are reported repeatedly, with descriptions that are often eerily similar—and the literature supports this—then you have to take a step back and question exactly what is going on. If these are not alien abductions, then what are they? What the hell is going on?

Women who experience such abduction scenarios involving hybrid babies are not only staggered by the experiences, but find themselves in a quandary. Do they keep quiet about what they experienced or do they tell their partners or family about it? Such an admission can be difficult and stressful, and possibly devastating for relationships.

Diane's husband started out as a complete skeptic, but in his decades with her has come around to believing that even though her experiences are rarely explicable, they are *real*. What she describes is *actually happening*.

Connie's husband was a skeptic until an incident occurred when they lived in the Georgia countryside. "Ted has always been an early riser and one morning he shook me awake, really excited. 'Connie, Connie wake up! Your friends are here! Look!'"

The barking dogs has prompted him to look out their bedroom window, which faced the backyard, meadow, woods, and a small barn that was close to the house. All five dogs were standing a few feet from the barn, yapping their heads off. "Three entities stood against the barn. One was about eight-feet tall or so, and two were about four-feet tall. They glanced over at the window, knew Ted was watching, stayed visible for a few seconds, then simply evaporated. The dogs instantly stopped barking. That experience opened his mind, but he doesn't like to talk about it because he feels crazy when he does. Before that incident, he had always laughed at me when I described my experiences. After that, he didn't laugh anymore."

It's easy to understand why a partner who has never experienced an encounter or abduction would be skeptical. Even in 2013, when decades of TV series, movies, books, and websites have primed our psyches for such things, our minds make careful divisions between entertainment and real life. Abductees also experience this kind of psychological division and with good reason.

First off, you're in a strange location and typically you don't remember how you got there. You're in a situation that is so strange to your points of reference that you're struggling to process it while it's happening. Little Gray beings hold you captive, stare into your eyes, paralyze you. They perform medical procedures on you, take your ovum, implant or remove something from your uterus, or ask you to hold and love a strange, deformed child that they tell you is yours. *Really?* And you're supposed to survive these types of experience *intact?*

Connie and Diane have never met face to face. They know each other only through our blog. Long before either of them came out publicly about their experiences, before they realized they were both abductees, they wrote to us privately about their experiences in the hybrid nursery. The parallels in their descriptions are stunning and coincide with what other abductees report about the nursery:

Dozens of fetuses float in tanks, completely immersed in a blue liquid, with wires of some kind attached to them. There's a humming noise in the room, presumably from the life support systems to which these fetuses are connected. They resemble human fetuses, but their eyes are huge, strange, dark.

Connie's memories of the nursery are vivid, omnipotent. She reported a "noxious, inhuman odor" that emanated from the nursery where she was taken. The fetuses she saw floated in a yellow liquid tinged with green and the foul odor also radiated from the infant she held. The odor, she says, was indescribable: sour sweet, warm, feverish, horrible. She has worked in hospital burn wards and the odor in these wards is strikingly similar to how these children smelled.

"It's simply, inhumanly awful. I haven't been taken there in a long while, but I always came back from that *baby place* overwhelmed with sadness and depression for days. They would put one of them in my arms and make me rock it and talk to it and it was just so soul-wrenching. The babies looked like tiny, wrinkled-up, ancient old folks, and they cried but made no sounds. Just tears. It was horrific."

In 1985, when Connie was 45, she was diagnosed with uterine cancer and had a radical hysterectomy. After that, the *texture* of her abductions changed. "There was no more probing of my private parts. It was then that they began to get in my face and seemed to create scenarios that they made me watch while they intensely monitored my reactions. And, the visits to the nursery became more frequent. I understand a psychiatrist would have a field day with this, saying I subconsciously wanted more children. But that is so not the case. They simply moved me along to a different type of situation that suited their agenda, whatever it was."

During one of Connie's visits to the nursery, she was standing in the center of a circular space and could see what appeared to be clear, transparent containers of some kind that looked like test tubes in a laboratory. They were large, stacked horizontally, not vertically, and held children of various ages.

"I remember being appalled because the containers seemed to have fluid in them and the babies were floating in the fluid. I also remember very vividly that every time a baby or young child—they were different ages—was put into my arms, it was wet with sticky stuff, and had that unholy, ungodly odor."

Connie didn't want to hold the babies, but didn't seem to have any choice. Once the infant was in her arms, she rocked it, talked to it, and wept. The babies seemed to be aware of her, aware of their environment, but didn't make a sound. Their eyes, she said, were tragically sad.

The nurseries were the worst part of all her abductions, particularly because that inhuman odor stayed with her for days afterward and nothing she did would get rid of it.

HARVESTING OF SOULS

Most researchers believe the reproductive procedures that occur during abductions are primarily a breeding program. The experiences that abductees report seem to support this conclusion. But if it's true, what's the larger purpose behind it?

"Because producing offspring is a primary goal of abductions, successful fetal implantation and extraction are critical," wrote David Jacobs in *The Threat: Revealing the Secret Alien Agenda*. "Without the fetal implantation-extraction phase of the program, the entire abduction phenomenon would be crippled, if not rendered inoperative." He believes the abduction phenomenon is overwhelmingly negative and concluded that hybrids or aliens will "integrate into human society and assume control..."

On this point, Jacobs differs from John Mack, who believed that the abduction phenomenon provides a venue for spiritual transformation. It is "one of a number of intrusions into our reality from other realms that are contributing to...the spiritual rebirth taking place in Western culture," he wrote in *Passport to the Cosmos: Human Transformation and Alien Encounters*. "It seems to have something to do with the human future."

Strieber is even more circumspect. From his 1987 *Communion* to *Solving the Communion Enigma,* written more than twenty years later, he seems to have reached a place of restless acceptance. Anger is absent from his later writings about his experiences. He has his theories, his suspicions, his beliefs. But he is still questioning, curious, engaged, probing, digging for the bottom line. What's obvious is his need to know what really happened to him, what it means for him personally, and what it might mean for us globally, for humanity. Through his prodigious writing skills, he attempts to stitch together a prototype that might prove helpful to the rest of us.

Diane says that it's difficult to know at any given time during an abduction what's actually going on or what you should do because *they* completely control the experience and take away your will to act. "When you're in the midst of these encounters, you don't have any thoughts about cameras, proof or evidence. There's always an implied threat to those you love, both human and animal. There's always ambiguity. I was never certain if the beings had any strictly physical presence. Your mind and perceptions are being messed with. You have no grounding. It's terrifying."

Author and researcher Karla Turner was far more skeptical about the hybrid scenario than other researchers. In an article entitled *Genetic Agenda a Double-Cross?* she noted, "There's no hybrid child yet in human custody. In every encounter, the human's total perceptive intake is controlled and frequently altered, easily manipulated to give the human a 'created' event to remember and a programmed set of tactile, emotional, and intellectual responses. That means that what we abductees think and what we remember of encounters may not accurately reflect the real events of the encounter."

Turner pointed out that crossbreeding isn't necessarily the alien agenda, that there could be other uses for the harvested genetic material— human clones or even the necessary DNA material to create Grays. The aliens themselves have provided contradictory explanations for their genetic program:

-They have to "upgrade" their dwindling race by creating a hybrid race.

-The human species has to be altered so that it can survive future catastrophes.

-They're serving God's plan by "preparing new bodies" for the return of Christ.

-They're producing clones of certain people so those individuals can be replaced.

"The evidence shows that the aliens do harvest from us in a number of ways, emotionally and energetically as well as psychically," Turner wrote in this same article.

In *Grey Aliens and the Harvesting of Souls: the Conspiracy to Genetically Tamper with Humanity,* author and researcher Nigel Kerner presents a complex cosmology to explain the motives of what he calls robotic entities involved in abductions. He begins with the premise that the Grays are artificially manufactured.

"It cannot have an opinion outside its programmed requisites," he wrote. "It *reasons* digitally and binomially, in terms of all previous permutations of information received. It will function in terms of mobility under a programmed drive to seek and maximize information, always, in all ways, information with one end, namely, the master command: *Protect your individuality at all costs so that you may protect your creator at all costs."*

The italicized section is intriguing, particularly the words *individuality* and *creator*. Individuality is not something that abductees usually associate with the Grays, who are described as clones, robots, machines, without feeling, a hive mentality. And when Kerner refers to creator, who is he talking about exactly? The ETs who control the Grays? A supreme being?

In Kerner's cosmology, the Grays long ago embarked on a constant search throughout the universe for DNA, so that they could create hybrids that would be able to reproduce. And by being able to reproduce, they would obtain what they're really after—a soul, a connection to something greater than themselves, a connection to God, Source, Godhead, whatever name you assign to a supreme being. So in the end, in Kerner's cosmology, the Grays are similar to Biblical fallen angels searching for redemption.

"What the Greys cannot understand is that access to eternal life is impossible for a Cloned being, as it has no direct connection to Godhead and can never have such a connection. They cannot understand this simply because they have no understanding of anything beyond the purely physical. Thus they abduct us, conduct experiments on sperms and ova, and create hybrid beings in the vain hope of somehow riding our souls into a capacity for birth."

Abductees often report that they didn't see any reproductive or sexual organs on the Grays, that they are asexual, with smooth genital areas, but that gender can sometimes be determined through an intuitive sense. *Her voice in my head is soft.... His eyes seized mine and won't let go...*

"I have spoken to a scientist from the Soviet Union," Kerner wrote, "who personally held a scalpel, who found this to be so. The seventeen alien bodies that have been found by the United States at the time of my research (his book was published in 2010) were identical to the one this Russian scientists worked on."

Blankets statements like these—without names or attribution—contribute to the fringe element in this field of research. Who was the Soviet scientist? Where are these seventeen alien bodies? How did the government gain possession of them? Please, spell it out.

Yet, there's a certain intuitive logic about the bigger picture of the theory that Kerner puts forth—that the Grays seek *a soul*. It's like what Diane Fine observed, *"They don't grok us."* She says: "They don't understand our emotional attachments to each other, to our animal companions, to our hopes and dreams. They don't understand our spiritual attachments and beliefs."

And perhaps that's because they are robots.

What we found depressing about Kerner's theories is that free will seems to be completely absent from the picture. When we asked Diane Fine why she thought these encounters had happened to her, she said they were part of what *she* had contracted for in this lifetime. Free will, in other words. *The soul's will.*

Comparisons have been made between the abduction experience and NDEs, between aliens and us in some undefined future. Whitley Strieber's Dreamland, his Internet radio show, explores these questions—and many others—but always from a surprisingly grounded and reasonable point of view. He is obviously a man in search of answers, but he isn't an alarmist like Kerner, who wrote: "A catastrophe greater than our species has faced in all its history awaits the human race today....Our universe spells doom and only doom."

One of the great mystics of the twentieth century was Jane Roberts, an Elmira, New York writer and poet. She channeled an entity called Seth, and together they wrote more than 20 books about the nature of reality. These books are dense, sometimes short on practicalities, but the core of the Seth material is simple: *You get what you concentrate on...there is no other main rule.*

If what Seth says is true, how might it fit into the abduction/UFO encounter scenario?

Abductees are terrified. Some part of these individuals, some part of their belief system, their psyche, has attracted this experience. That terror can be used as a launch pad into an exploration, an expansion of consciousness, a spiritual epiphany. Or it can be used to perpetuate more terror and uncertainty. In the end, our experiences and how we assimilate them are subject to free will. All too often, abductees become enablers, hiding their experiences, too fearful to act. But suppose they became activists, speaking out as a group? How would that change things?

HYBRIDS AMONG US

Whatever the ultimate goal in the abduction phenomenon, let's go along with the majority of researchers for a moment and speculate about what these hybrids might look like, if they exist.

Connie's theory about children with progeria is based upon her own experiences. Year ago, she saw her first live interview on a TV talk show with a child who had progeria. "I was stunned by the resemblance between these children and the hybrid children on the crafts with whom I was forced to interact."

About one in every eight million children in the world have progeria. It's considered to be a genetic mutation, but scientists haven't been able to find the gene that causes the mutation. Connie believes that children with progeria are actually embryos left in situ in the womb, to gestation and birth, as opposed to being 'harvested' and taken to the hybrid nurseries. Essentially, she believes it's a failed experiment, hybrid insemination gone awry.

"The resemblance to the aliens is simply too detailed, and the progress of progeria suggests some type of artificial insemination yet to be discovered by our most diligent medical researchers."

What about adult hybrids? Are they here among us? Linda, a writer who lives in Nevada, believes she had an experience with such a being. The incident occurred ten to twelve years ago, in the parking lot of a grocery store in Reno.

She and her husband were out running errands and stopped at the grocery store. "I jumped out of the car to run inside the store and grab what I needed. Walking toward me was a man with longish black hair. When I passed him I glanced up at his face and his eyes were *black*. The hair stood up all over my body and the words—*mass murderer, evil*—popped into my head."

Linda couldn't shake the feeling and as soon as she got back into the car, told her husband about it. "I was recently reminded of this incident while listening to Whitley Strieber talking about black-eyed people on his radio show, *Dreamland*. I've never had such a visceral reaction to someone in my entire life. I have never forgotten about it. I had the exact same reaction as many others have had when confronted by these beings. I do not believe they are human."

Linda's story intrigued us, especially since Charles Fontaine had told us of a similar experience he had. It happened more than a year after the initial encounter in his backyard and, like Linda's experience, occurred in a grocery store parking lot.

On the evening of May 3, 2012, Charles was sitting behind the steering wheel of his car, the map light turned on, as he looked for the receipt for the groceries that he had just put in the trunk. "Seemingly from nowhere, a strange person appeared on my left. He or she was very tall, thin, bald, with extremely white skin and very small ankles." The individual was dressed entirely in blue, wearing strange pants—like baseball pants that were tight at the ankles—and held an armful of grocery bags in one hand.

Charles watched the person move past his car on the left. "He walked like an insect. Or like an ant in a cartoon." Even though it was night, the man wore dark, square sunglasses. As Charles continued to watch, the person suddenly looked toward him and abruptly changed directions, stepping out in front of his car. "I didn't like it and felt sorry for him. I thought the poor person must be handicapped."

Charles started his car, but decided to wait before moving forward so as not to frighten the person. But as he waited, the man started moving toward him, "walking like a robot from a science fiction movie."

The longer Charles watched, the more uneasy he became. There was something aggressive in the way the man looked at him and Charles had the distinct feeling that he wasn't grocery shopping, but was in that parking lot to find *him*.

The windows in the car were raised, but even so, Charles could hear the person screaming in a language he couldn't identify. "It was like the sounds cats make when they fight." It freaked him out and he decided he'd better get out of there.

As Charles began driving slowly ahead, the man lunged toward his car. Charles stopped so he wouldn't hit the person, who then leaned over his windshield and tried to communicate with that weird, screeching sound. Although the man didn't touch the car, Charles was terrified he would try to open his car door. So Charles started driving forward again.

"That's when I realized that he couldn't walk or move his hands in an ordinary way. I looked over my shoulder to see what he was doing and saw that he was looking at the back of my car, still making those weird sounds."

Shaken by the encounter, Charles sped away. "I still don't like thinking about this person. I'm afraid he'll come back into my life someday. Yet, I've been questioning myself ever since. Was I just being afraid of a handicapped person? Why would he be carrying so many grocery bags? How would he possibly carry so many bags of groceries home? I couldn't help wondering if this person was a human-alien hybrid."

When you Google black-eyed children, you find all kinds of strange and frightening stories about them. They're like the weird kids in *Village of the Damned,* the result of alien/human breeding, gifted with supernatural powers. The way the person moved, insect-like, reminded us of the so-called man in black who appeared at our sliding glass door late at night in Fort Lauderdale (chapter 3) when we were talking about related matters with several people, including an abductee.

Connie used to attend a spiritual group held at a local metaphysical shop. One night after the meeting, the owner introduced her to Anna. Connie remembers noticing her before the meeting and thinking that she looked like an alien. She had the appearance of an adult child with progeria, but was in her thirties. Yet, children afflicted with this condition usually die by puberty.

Connie described Anna as short, barely five feet tall. She wore a dark wig, her forehead was protuberant and her head was too large for her body. "I remember wondering how such a thin neck held up such a large head."

Anna's eyes were wide set, large, black and dull, like coal. She had a tiny nose, and a slit for a mouth. The texture of her skin appeared rough, the color was pasty, "like a person with a severe heart condition or with a limited oxygen level in the blood. Essentially, she looked like a 'tall' Gray dressed as a human."

Anna was oddly reticent. She spoke only when spoken to and then only briefly. Her voice, Connie recalls, was quite hoarse. She later learned the hoarseness was due to drugs that had been administered to her during certain experiments, that Anna and her daughter were on the run and rarely stayed in one place too long.

At the time, Connie was giving psychic consultations and Anna subsequently made three appointments with her. Each time, though, she refused to meet Connie at her home, despite her assurances that her house was safe. She insisted they meet in a public place and eventually told Connie that her father was a colonel in the American military and that he had allowed her to be used in alien experiments.

What does that mean, though? Was she a hybrid? Was she on the run from the military, from the Grays, or both? It's easy to dismiss such stories, but Connie sensed Anna was sincere.

"She told me she had been on a base in Germany, then a base in the Southwest somewhere, from which she and her daughter had managed to escape. She described some of the things that had been done to her, drugs she'd been given, procedures she'd endured. Her body reflected the truth of everything she told me. I saw the scars. Her terror at being found was palpable. Even though a surgeon had removed a tracking device implanted behind her ear, she remained petrified they would find her. And if they did, she feared they would kill her."

Even though Anna's young daughter looked perfectly normal, Anna was convinced that she too had been altered some way and might have a tracking device implanted in her. Nonetheless, Anna and her daughter kept running.

After their third meeting, Connie never saw her again. "I worried about her and asked the shop owner if she had any news. It's my hope that she got away. But I suspect they found her."

The military involvement in Anna's story wouldn't have surprised Karla Turner. Speaking at a MUFON (Mutual UFO Network) conference in the mid-'90s, she said: "Since at least 1947, a power structure within the military intelligence has appropriated the UFO phenomenon, has made it their own sphere. We're the 'sheeple.' Our leaders don't want us to know what's going on."

In *A.D.: After Disclosure*, authors Richard M. Dolan and Bryce Zabel argue that the Grays may be "a type of cybernetic life form." Perhaps they're programmed to abduct humans "and bioengineer bodies that would allow them to colonize. Such a plan would take quite a few generations, maybe even centuries. Patience may be their dominant trait."

If any of this is true, how long will the silence, the dismissal, the disinformation, go on? We'll take a look at that question in the next chapter.

CHAPTER 8
WHAT'S COMING

Disclosure: the revelation that they are here, that they have been here, and some in power have known about it a long time.

PRESIDENTS AND UFOS

E very president of the United States over the past 50 years has been asked what he knows about UFOs. The answer is always the same. He never has been told anything about the subject. Are they all hiding something? Maybe, but more than likely they aren't. They might be as out of the loop on this extraordinary subject as the rest of us. Possibly there's a group hidden somewhere in the government or military that deals exclusively with the subject and one of their goals is to keep the public in the dark about the greatest secret of our time.

On several occasions, Ronald Reagan talked about how humanity would be united by the arrival of aliens. Speaking before the United Nations on Sept. 21, 1987, he said: "I occasionally think how quickly our differences worldwide would vanish if we were facing an alien threat from outside this world. And yet, I ask is not an alien force *already* among us?" He quickly clarified the last comment, or turned the last comment into a double entendre, when he added that he was referring to war and the threat of war.

On June 27, 1982, Reagan invited Steven Spielberg to the White House for a private screening of *E.T.: The Extraterrestrial*. Thirty-five other people attended, including Supreme Court Judge Sandra Day O'Connor. The movie was shown in the White House theater after a reception in the Blue Room and dinner in the Red Room. The Reagans were captivated by the movie and afterwards, Reagan supposedly leaned over to Spielberg and whispered, "You know, there aren't six people in this room who know how true this really is." Several people approached and Spielberg never had a chance to question the president about the comment.

Bill Clinton allegedly began his presidency by asking two questions: *who killed JFK and are there UFOs?* Bill and Hillary spoke openly about UFOs. During his presidency, UFOs were mentioned on 26 occasions, far more than any previous president. In 1995, following a speech in Belfast, Ireland, Clinton said that if the U.S. Air Force had captured a UFO at Roswell, no one had informed him of that fact.

A CIA scientist was asked to provide a briefing on the UFO question for Clinton's science advisor. A friend of the scientist commented, "It was known among the high CIA people, and the people who had contact with these people (the Clintons) that they were on the prowl for UFOs. He (Bill) had been asking anyone who would listen to him, to tell him the secret. You know, he would get some admiral in there, and say, "By the way, tell me the UFO secret."

In 2005, after Clinton had left office, he made a speech to a financial group in Hong Kong. In a question and answer period afterward, he was asked about secrets that were passed from president to president.

"Well I don't know if you all heard this, but, there was actually, when I was president in my second term, there was an anniversary observance of Roswell. Remember that? People came to Roswell, New Mexico from all over the world. And there was also a site in Nevada where people were convinced that the government had buried a UFO and perhaps an alien deep underground because we wouldn't allow anybody to go there. And um… I can say now, 'cause it's now been released into the public domain…. This place in Nevada was really serious, that there was an alien artifact there. So I actually sent somebody there to figure it out.

"I did attempt to find out if there were any secret government documents that revealed things. If there were, they were concealed from me too. And if there were, well, I wouldn't be the first American president that underlings have lied to, or that career bureaucrats have waited out. But there may be some career person sitting around somewhere, hiding these dark secrets, even from elected presidents. But if so, they successfully eluded me…and I'm almost embarrassed to tell you I did (chuckling) try to find out."

In October 1969, when Jimmy Carter was still a private citizen, he had a UFO sighting. He reported it in 1973 to the International UFO Bureau in Oklahoma City. He was governor of Georgia at the time, and he remains the only president to have filed such a UFO report.

His sighting occurred shortly after dark, on a clear, windless night.

He was outside the Lion's Club in Leary, Georgia, waiting for a meeting to start when, quite suddenly, he and ten or more witnesses, saw a luminous object. "It seemed to move toward us from a distance, stop, move partially away, return, then depart. Bluish at first, then reddish... At times, it was as bright as the moon and about as big as the moon—maybe a bit smaller."

Carter believed the object was three hundred to a thousand yards away, and that the sighting lasted for at least ten minutes. In an interview with the *Atlanta Constitution,* Carter described the sighting as "remarkable" and talked about it numerous times over the years.

His mother, Lillian, confirmed that Carter was impressed by what he'd seen. "The UFO made a huge impression on Jimmy. He told me about the sighting many times. He's always been a down-to-earth no-nonsense boy, and the sighting by him, as far as I am concerned, is as firm as money in the bank."

Skeptics, however, doubted Carter's claim. Robert Sheaffer of the Scientific Investigation of Claims of the Paranormal—SCICOP- wrote in the July 1977 issue of *Humanist Magazine* that Carter probably had spotted Venus. It's true that Venus is the brightest object in the sky besides the moon. But it seems doubtful that someone in the group with Carter wouldn't have recognized the planet. Sheaffer didn't explain how the planet seemed to move and appeared less than 1,000 yards away.

In spite of his sighting, video exists where Carter says he doesn't believe "space people" have visited Earth and that he doesn't think it's even possible.

This contradiction is typical for just about everything connected to UFOs and aliens. The entire topic is a minefield. No matter where you step, where you drill, the explosion of information makes it difficult to connect the dots. Truth is mixed in with disinformation, outright lies, distortions, myths.

The April 25, 1988 issue of *The New Yorker* carried an interview with Senator Barry Goldwater, a former presidential candidate who was deeply interested in UFOs. He said he repeatedly asked his friend, General Curtis LeMay, if there was any truth to the rumors that UFO evidence was stored in a secret room at Wright-Patterson Air Force Base. Goldwater also asked if he could gain access to that room. According to Goldwater, an angry LeMay gave him "holy hell" and said, "Not only can't you get into it, but don't you ever mention it to me again."

Goldwater talks about the exchange in a videotaped interview on You Tube. The conservative Republican, who was at the top of his party's presidential ticket in 1964, apparently was convinced the government was protecting a secret and hiding the evidence at Wright-Patterson Air Force Base.

While transparency in government is praised in democracies, exposing secrets is usually considered treacherous and treasonous. This apparent contradiction is flagrant when it comes to the subject of UFOs.

In *A.D.: After Disclosure,* authors Dolan and Zabel speculate about who or what is or has been in charge of secrecy regarding UFOs. "When Disclosure finally comes in the future, it will reveal the existence of a group that has pulled the strings on the UFO secrets for years. It probably has a name, one that we are unaware of now, that will be exposed and become infamous."

They refer to this cabal of secret-keepers as the Breakaway Group. "Bolstered by tremendous co-opted assets worldwide," this group of men and women doesn't answer to any political or military authority, not even to the president of the U.S. Whatever name we give this gang, they are and have been for nearly 70 years, the ET power brokers.

STRATEGY

Colonel Philip J Corso, a former Pentagon official who wrote *The Day After Roswell*, includes a chapter in his book called "The Strategy." This chapter in his book, published in 1997 by Pocket Books, is one of the best explanations we've found about how Roswell and other UFO-related matters since then have been kept secret for so long:

"Were you to search through every government document to find the declassified secrets of Roswell and the contact we maintained with the aliens who were visiting us before and have been doing so ever since, you would find code-named project after code-named project, each with its own file, security classification, military or government administration, oversight mechanism, some sort of budget, and even reports of highly classified documents. All of these projects were started to accomplish part of the same task: manage our ongoing relationship with the alien visitors we discovered at Roswell. However, at each level, once the security had been breached for whatever reason—even by design—part of the secret was disclosed through declassification while the rest was dragged into a new classified project or moved to an existing one that had not been compromised."

This stunning insight into how a government maintains secrets actually makes perfect sense. As a piece of one secret is uncovered, those in the know declassify the documents pertaining to that piece of the secret, then scramble to put the rest of the secret into a new little box with a new name and new classification. "For all the years after Roswell," Corso writes, "we weren't just one step ahead of people wanting to know what really happened, we were a hundred steps ahead, a thousand, or even more. In fact, we never hid the truth from anybody, we just camouflaged it. It was always there, people just didn't know what to look for or recognize it for what it was when they found it. And they found it over and over again."

Corso's statements, of course, have been refuted by others, such as John B. Alexander, a retired army colonel and government insider. In his book, *UFOs: Myths, Conspiracies, and Realities*, he includes a chapter called "The Corso Conundrum," in which he details everything that's wrong with Corso's version of events.

"Corso made many extraordinary claims, especially regarding the use of crashed UFO material in the development of American advanced technology. Unfortunately, none of those claims have been substantiated, and most are directly refuted by known facts." After the publication of Corso's book, Alexander wrote Corso a seven-page letter addressing the errors he'd found.

Alexander takes a moderate position on UFOs, contending that there are unknown objects traversing our skies that seem to be under intelligent control. He's well aware that many people are fearful of talking about their sightings or encounters, that scientists avoid the topic, fearing ridicule. He realizes that skeptics make deductions about UFO sightings that are not founded on evidence, and make personal attacks on those who come forward with their stories.

On the other hand, Alexander doubts there is a secret government conspiracy to hide the facts, as Corso and others contend. In fact, he tends to blame overly enthusiastic UFO researchers for obscuring the matter by creating legends, myths and conspiracies.

Yet, the official government MO for the last 66 years has been cover-up, denial, and disinformation. If you doubt that the U.S. government has attempted to hide information or deceive the public about UFOs, drop by a website called The Black Vault. Run by John Greenewald, Jr., The Black Vault includes more than 600,000 pages of declassified material released under the Freedom of Information Act (FOIA).

For a government with an official stance that UFOs do not exist, it's staggering to see how often the topic appears in official documents. In 2009, the CIA released multiple documents after a request was filed with the Defense Intelligence Agency. Next to the PDF file for these documents, Greenewald noted that the 65 pages released "prove the CIA is still collecting intelligence in regards to UFOs, and that material from just the past few years is considered a threat to our national security."

One document from the president's Office of Science and Technology Policy labeled "UFO strategy" discusses efforts to curtail comments about UFO-related technology on a so-called 'open government blog' sites created to attract ideas from the public. The UFO-related comments were categorized as *fringe ideas* and were removed from the main discussion. Staff members, in e-mail exchanges, discussed the irony of blocking UFO comments while promoting open public discussion.

One of the memos noted: "*The New York Times*, however, is reporting that while the Obama administration has asked the public for new ideas with the unveiling of an open-government website, the administration is considering steps to curtail free speech and discussion of the UFO issue on the prejudiced supposition that UFO subjects are somehow 'fringe'—the modern term for heresy, which was considered a crime against the church when Galileo published his findings in opposition to the conventional wisdom of his time."

In browsing documents in The Black Vault, it quickly becomes obvious that the U.S. government is like a huge squid with so many tentacles that no single arm has the full information on UFOs. Different agencies possess bits and pieces of the puzzle and it's easy to imagine administrators scrambling to uncover what the other agencies know—or don't know. If that's the case, and no one group holds all the information, how will disclosure ever happen?

Many UFO researchers believe that full disclosure most likely will occur in the aftermath of an event or events—such as mass sightings that will overpower the ability of government to dismiss UFOs and aliens as fiction, as nonsense, as a joke. However, we've had mass sightings already—The Phoenix Lights, The Hudson Valley sightings—so this mass sighting would have to be enormous, perhaps simultaneous sightings worldwide that are photographed and videotaped by thousands. In an era of Smart phones with high definition video capabilities, this possibility is certainly plausible. If and when that day comes, our beliefs about the nature of reality will shift violently. We will no longer be able to claim we are the most advanced beings on the planet.

As Ronald Reagan predicted, we might unite as humans as never before. But we might also face an enemy capable of destroying us, an enemy who knows far more about us than we know about it. An enemy who might want to decimate the human race in order to save the planet.

It seems we are collectively preparing ourselves for disclosure, subtly shifting our awareness through popular culture. We've gone from the lovable child-like alien in *ET* to the insidious and hostile image of the black-eyed Gray first depicted on the cover of Whitley Strieber's 1987 bestseller *Communion*.

WHAT DOES THE GOVERNMENT KNOW?

In 2009, we were invited to a book festival in St. Augustine, Florida, the country's oldest city. These festivals are always fun and a great venue for meeting publishers, agents, and other writers. The deeper value of these events for us is connecting with individuals who share our metaphysical interests. It turned out that the woman who put the festival together, Jewell Bradfield Kutzer, was an ordained minister in a local science of mind church and has had a wide spectrum of experiences.

We communicated sporadically for the next three years, mostly about synchronicity, which we were writing about at the time. We didn't realize she'd had any encounters or sightings until we mentioned that we were writing a book about alien abductees, which included some of the experiences of an abductee from St. Augustine. We asked her if she knew Connie Cannon and emailed Connie and asked if she knew Jewell. It turned out they not only knew each other, but that Connie used to attend Jewell's services years earlier. They had fallen out of touch.

Spurred on by the synchronicity, we asked Jewell if she'd ever had an encounter. Her reply led us back to 1961, the same year of the Betty and Barney Hill abduction. "My husband was an engineer with the US Army Corps of Engineers. In early 1961, he was sent to work at the Florida facility that was building the original launch pads for what would become the space program at Cape Canaveral."

The Canaveral area and all their operations at the time fell under the auspices of Patrick Air Force Base, which is located just south of Cocoa Beach, in the Canaveral area, on Florida's east coast. In those early years of missile launches, Jewell said, more of them *blew up* than *went up*. "But it was a hub of frantic activity as the U.S. government sought to win the space race."

One evening Jewell and Charles were driving along U.S. 1 going north where the highway paralleled the Indian River, adjacent to the Canaveral missile test area to the east. Charles suddenly yelled out, *"Jewell, look!"* He pointed in the direction of the river, immediately pulled over to the right side of the road, stopped, and they got out of their car.

"Hovering over the river was a round or elliptical object that was illuminated. It made no sound but its lights were very visible. As we watched, all of a sudden it took off to the north at a tremendous speed—faster than I had ever seen any plane move. And then, just as abruptly, it stopped on a dime."

Once again, it hovered over the river near the far bank. Jewell and Charles watched it for a moment, speculating about what it might be. "Then it suddenly took off again at a dramatic speed and stopped once more just as suddenly. It repeated these kind of maneuvers for several minutes, and then shot away, out across the test area and over the Atlantic and disappeared."

Charles knew exactly how to react to this sighting, Jewell said. He and all the other engineers working in the area had been issued cards that provided a phone number to call whenever a sighting occurred. "The sightings were so frequent in those days they had enlisted everybody's help to keep track of them. When we got home, Charles called in the information and asked if anyone else had reported the event. The man on the phone said that they couldn't give him that information."

However, the next day Charles found out that five or six other people in his division had also sighted the object and reported it. Charles and Jewell assumed that the calls were being recorded by someone at Patrick Air Force Base.

The general scuttlebutt at the time was that it was some kind of Russian plane and that the Russians were checking out what the U.S. was doing with their space program. "That idea was scary enough," Jewell said. "But to the best of my knowledge Russia never achieved such a capability—nor, I believe, have we. That evening is seared into my brain."

A few years ago, Jewell had the opportunity to talk with a woman who was one of the first women permitted in the launch facilities. She verified that she also had been given a card with information on it on how to report any mysterious sightings."

So what did the government know then, just fourteen years after the alleged crash at Roswell? What would prompt them to issue such cards to the employees at Cape Canaveral?

GOVERNMENT SPYING

We initially posted Charles Fontaine's experience in nine segments on our blog. From the day the first post went up, our statistics counter started logging visits from government agencies. By the time the ninth piece of the story was posted, we'd had visits from: the Department of Defense, the FBI, the U.S. Department of Defense Network Information System, the Navy Network Information Center (NINC), the Federal Communications Commission (FCC), the Department of Defense Network, (DOD) the Social Security Administration (that one is really puzzling: social security for aging aliens?) the 754th Electronic Systems Group, and the Royal Canadian Mounted Police.

Let's take a closer look at these last two organizations. The 754th ELSG operates out of Maxwell Air Force base in Alabama and, according to the air force, "provides responsive information systems to support more efficient and effective logistics, contracting and comm-computer capabilities Air Force wide." The 754th promotional guide notes that their mission is "... to fly and fight in Air, Space and Cyberspace." In other words, they're surveilling the skies and patrolling the Internet.

The Royal Canadian Mounted Police—RCMP—is the Canadian national police force—comparable to the FBI—and someone from there spent eight hours on our blog, sifting through all the posts and comments. It's as if an employee had been assigned to keep tabs. Why?

Canada, like a few other countries, has begun releasing its UFO files. But their official stance parallels that of the U.S.—that in most cases, UFO sightings are explicable and attributable to flares and birds and weird light refractions in camera lenses. So why were government departments in both countries interested in the Quebec encounters?

These spy agencies often use a browser called *Rippers*. We'd never heard of it until it started appearing in our counter. Rippers is apparently a browsing software that enables the user to copy an entire blog or website and view it offline. Why? What threat could this information possibly pose to the national security of either country?

It's not the information so much as the implications that result from it. If the reports about the ways in which crafts move and manipulate themselves are true, if it's true that citizens are being whisked up into alien ships, then the U.S. and Canadian military forces are unable to protect their citizens or the airspace over their respective countries. Maybe that fact is already known and has been known for decades. Maybe they have even formed an alliance, one that allows aliens to conduct discreet abductions in exchange for keeping their presence a secret.

It sounds like science fiction. But what if a highly secretive element of the U.S. military and government is complicit in some abduction cases? When Connie and her son ended up on Warner Robins Air Force base, she's certain she witnessed aliens co-mingling with Air Force personnel. An experience that Diane Fine had in the early 1990s seems to support this as well.

In December 1992, Diane was part of a twelve-person committee that sponsored the first US-Soviet symposium on UFOs. It was held at the University of California at Berkeley, under the direction of Dr. James Harder, professor emeritus at Berkeley who taught civil and hydraulic engineering. Harder was also known as a prominent UFO researcher who studied the subject for more than fifty years. He investigated the abduction of Betty and Barney Hill in 1961 and the abduction and five-day disappearance of Travis Walton in 1975. In 1968, Harder was one of six scientists to testify on UFOs before the U.S. House of Representatives Committee on Science and Aeronautics.

The week-long symposium Diane was involved in featured a number of speakers, among them Dr. Steven Greer, Colin Andrews, and the highly decorated Russian test pilot Dr. Marina Popovich. Diane's job during that week was to stick close to Popovich, one of the most important female pilots of all time, who held 107 aviation records. But in UFO circles, Popovich is famous because she's an aviation legend who is also a *believer.*

In her books and speeches, Popovich has mentioned the more than 3,000 sightings by Soviet military and civilian pilots and claims that the Soviet Air Force and KGB have pieces of five crashed UFOs in their possession. In December 1991, Popovich revealed a photo she claimed was given to her by cosmonaut Alexei Leonov, the first man to walk in space and also a high official in the Soviet space program. She said she had smuggled it out of the former USSR. It showed a UFO hovering near the moon Phobos, and was apparently the cause of the disappearance of the Soviet's Phobos 2 probe, which sent back 37 images before it vanished. The photo was shown at a press conference held at the Russian Consulate in San Francisco during the week of the symposium.

On the last Sunday of the event, Popovich, Andrew and Greer sat on a panel at Berkeley, answering questions from the public. Diane was acting as a hostess and was organizing and sending out press releases during this event. She was a Navy wife at the time and her husband's chain of command had been harassing her about her involvement in the symposium.

"I was so naïve. I kept saying it was my constitutional right to talk about anything I wanted. But it was during this time that our phones were tapped, government vehicles followed my car, my home was broken into, and my dog was hung. I was living in South Napa then, working with Harder and also working at a marina."

During the week of the symposium, black unmarked helicopters relentlessly buzzed the marina where Diane worked. 'Angel hair' fell from the sky on the marina's grounds. It's a sticky, fibrous substance like the threads of a spider web that is usually linked to UFO scenarios and disappears within minutes. None of it surprised Diane. By this point in her life, she had already been through numerous abductions, had experienced a "missing pregnancy," had met the ETs face to face and believed, for the most part, that they were not nice guys. Like other experiencers, she believed the military was covering up the truth.

As John Mack noted in his book *Abduction*, "For our own government and other governments around the world the abduction phenomenon presents a special problem. It is, after all, the *business* of government to protect its people, and for officials to acknowledge that strange beings from radar-defying craft can, in seeming defiance of the laws of gravity and space/time itself, invade our homes and abduct our people creates particular problems. This may explain why the government policy in relation to UFOs has been, from the beginning, so confusing, a kind of garbled mixture of denial and cover-up that only fuels conspiracy theories."

It's almost as if the characters depicted by Tommy Lee Jones and Will Smith in the MIB movies aren't too far from the truth. Perhaps Hollywood movies are the modern day expression of the collective mind, the myths and legends about UFOs and aliens. From the *MIB* movies to *ET, Independence Day* and *Ender's Game*, from *X-Files* to *V* to *4400* to *Falling Skies*, we have been fed many of the possible scenarios about UFOs and aliens. Are any of them true? Do any of them possess elements of truth? What do we actually know?

DREAMS OF DISCLOSURE

A recent poll by the National Geographic Society indicated that 36 percent of Americans—about 80 million people—believe that UFOs exist; 77 percent believe there are signs that aliens have visited our planet; and that 80 percent of Americans believe the government is hiding information about UFOs. So it's not surprising that many people are also dreaming about UFOs.

A typical dream might involve aliens arriving on spaceships, spaceships filling the sky, or one enormous craft. There might be a sense of the end of the world, aliens influencing our thoughts and actions, or widespread panic.

Some of these dreams could be metaphors for other issues in your life. A UFO or alien dream might symbolize a feeling of alienation and prompt you to ask from whom or what do you feel alienated? Carl Jung believed that dreams of flying saucers were predicting the outbreak of World War II, but also saw them as mandalas that symbolized a desire for wholeness or a spiritual search.

That could be the case with this dream sent to us by Dale Dassel, who lives near Macon, Georgia. "A couple weeks ago, I had a dream where I saw a UFO hovering motionless in the sky in broad daylight. Instead of the usual disc or triangle, it was a ring-shaped craft with a reflective plate in the center, rather like a dark gray donut with a mirror blocking the hole, and many small dark windows dotting its circumference. I've never seen a UFO like that in any book or movie, but it was really unique and cool-looking. Of course, I probably wouldn't say that if I saw it in real life; I'd probably be galvanized with terror and awe."

Other UFO dreams might be premonitions of disclosure. Or, they could be both symbolic or a precognitive. When we mentioned to Dale that we were wondering how common UFO dreams are becoming, he recalled a recurring UFO dream involving a mass landing at night.

In that dream, he said, the ground was covered with luminescent holograms rather like the Nazca lines in Peru, which projected into the sky to guide the ships down. The ships were of myriad shapes, impossibly gigantic, and there were literally thousands of them, almost like a colonization force.

"I remember feeling really exhilarated during the dream; being simultaneously excited and terrified. When I woke, my pulse was racing and the imagery was vividly clear in my mind. Part of me wanted the scenario to be real, while the other part desperately hoped it would never happen. But I haven't had that dream in quite awhile, so hopefully it wasn't prescient."

The feeling of exhilaration is a common sensation during dreams of UFOs—especially a large vessel filling the sky or many small ones.

Mike Clelland of Idaho, who blogs about UFOs on his site, *Hidden Experience*, recalls one such dream from Feb. 16, 2010 that he described as 'weirdly vivid.' It occurred the night before he would begin a long drive to Laughlin, Nevada for a UFO conference. So the subject was on his mind.

"My sleep was restless, and since I had my laptop near my bed, I listened to an audio podcast to occupy my time. Shortly after starting the podcast, I fell asleep. The dream begins in a nighttime environment, and I'm standing in a gravel parking lot—or a gravel road in a very distinctive forest. The pine trees are evenly spaced, and there are no branches down low.

"The forest floor is flat, without any undergrowth. I look to my left and see a very weird orange light shining through the trees. I move a little closer to get a better view, and see that it's a simple lampshade set on the ground, or maybe floating a few inches above the ground. It emits a vibrant orange glow. Instantly, I have the thought that this is *not* a lampshade, it's some sort of hallucination, and something else is there."

Even in his dream state, Mike thought about an event in Dr. Karla Turner's book, *Into the Fringe*. "There was a creepy scene in that book where a witness describes seeing a 'satellite dish' in his yard, but he knows it's *not* a satellite dish."

He looks at the lampshade for just a few seconds, and then finds himself floating up off the forest floor. "I rise up, slow and smooth, and I think to myself: *Oh, this again.* My perception is that the experience is quite familiar, and actually very pleasant. This comforting feeling fits a pattern of what I call my reassuring dreams."

Soon he is levitating above the tall trees and looking down into the pine forest. His floating body is positioned with a slight tilt forward, so he's forced to look downward. Below him is a huge round circle, inky black against a pale orange glow among the trees. He realizes it's a large saucer-shaped craft, and he smoothly descends toward it.

Then he discovers he is floating in a shiny glowing blue tube, and slowly descending. The walls of the tube are covered with a collection of brightly colored puzzle pieces inlaid in the wall. These shapes looks somewhat like Egyptian hieroglyphs. They seem to be made of candy-colored plastic and are backlit inside a frame.

"I'm reminded of a brightly colored child's toy. I reach forward and pick out one puzzle piece. It's as if I'm drawn to this one shape. I hold it in my hand and examine it closely. It is shaped like a stylized 'W' and I'm filled with an intense compulsion to remember it. I continue down into the tube, and then I'm walking around in a series of blue rooms crowded with people."

The dream seems to culminate with a meeting in a daylight street scene. "I'm in a crowd of people, and there is a discussion by a small team. They are carefully explaining that everything is all right and that there will soon be a wonderful event where UFO occupants will join us here on earth.

"It sounds logical and nice, but it seems a little too perfect. I approach the woman sharing the story, and tell her that I don't believe her, that my intuition senses some sort of deception. Suddenly her eyes get big and black, and the same thing happens with her teammates. She stares at me in a very threatening way and warns me NOT to tell anyone about my feelings."

That's when he woke up.

This last segment of Mike's dream bears eerie parallels to what Connie Cannon and her son experienced on Warner-Robbins Air Force Base. Although Connie was awake and driving at the outset of the incident, the experience took on a dreamlike scenario as she found herself and her son threatened by a military man while Grays hover nearby. It's also similar to Diane Fine's experience with the rock star who turned out to be a shift-shifting alien.

All of these experiences and dreams scream for resolution: what is the true nature of reality? Who are we in the greater scheme of things? What's really going on? Are we being primed for disclosure—or, as author Nigel Kerner believes—the complete takeover of the human race by nefarious ETs? It's why we have to pay attention to these dreams, to these abductees, to the minute details of what happened when.

After Mike recorded his dream, he turned off the light. In the dark he saw a small floating blue orb about the size of a grapefruit, centered in the ceiling above his bed. "I saw it for probably less than twenty seconds and then it was gone. It disappeared quickly and smoothly. Right after it faded away, I rolled over and promptly went to sleep, an unusual reaction to seeing something so strange."

He described the orb as sphere-shaped, rather than flat, and glowing softly. He wondered if it could have been an image created in his retina by his bedside light. He tried to recreate the experience by looking into lights in the room, including the tiny red light on the voice recorder, and then shutting the lights off. But these efforts didn't create any images even close to what he saw that night.

Dreams of abductions don't necessarily mean that the dreamer has been abducted. It could be a symbolic dream, a concern about being required to do something you wish you weren't doing. The image comes to mind because alien abduction stories have been widely publicized. However, when such a dream occurred before abductions became widely known, the issue is more puzzling.

That was the case with Sharlie West of Maryland, who years ago—long before she read anything about alien abductions—dreamed she was inside a spaceship.

"Everything was gray. No color at all. The spacemen were not human, and looked like pictures I later saw—steel gray, small, slanted black holes where eyes would be. I was on what looked like a hospital bed and realized they wanted to experiment on me. They communicated telepathically, but they were totally impersonal and about to dissect me in some way. They said: *We are able to enter your dreams whenever we want. That's how we manage things.* That gave me an uncomfortable feeling of invasion, and I ran to escape them. They chased after me and were closely on my heels when I woke up."

Stunned and frightened, she didn't know what to think about the dream. But ever since, Sharlie has had a negative feeling about aliens. "They are *not* our friends. Possibly it was just a dream, my imagination. Who knows? But I still have that feeling of waiting for the other shoe to drop."

Sharlie related her abduction dream after telling us about a series of recent dreams. "I've had three strange dreams in the last week about aliens among us. They look like the rest of us, but are infiltrating everywhere. They are unobtrusive, their purpose is difficult to determine."

Sharlie recognized that her dream could be symbolic. "If it's not literally true, I'm wondering if these beings are metaphors for an unseen threat to the U.S., a calm before a storm."

What if both explanations are true?

In 2011, Bruce Gernon had an extremely vivid dream. He was at an airshow when a massive UFO appeared in the sky above a crowd, put on quite a spectacle, and revealed the existence of life from beyond this world.

"My friend Kathy Doore loaned me an ancient carved stone that came from Markawasi, Peru. She said it was enchanted and sacred, like the site itself. It featured a strange-looking bird with a lizard's tail on it. She told me to put it under my pillow when I go to sleep and I would dream something special. I tried it and absolutely nothing special happened. I had the same type of boring and senseless dreams I usually have."

Three days later, Bruce returned the stone to Kathy. But the next morning, just as he woke up, he had an incredibly vivid vision about a space ship. He noted that he had never experienced any such visions or dreams about UFOs.

"We were at a large gathering of tens of thousands of people. It might have been an air show like the one every year at Lakeland, Florida. It was at night and the show was just ending when this incredible event took place. Out of nowhere, a gigantic space ship appeared directly overhead and hovered about 500 feet above us. It was about 500 feet long and 250 feet wide. It looked similar in shape to the famous Star Trek space ship except it was more streamlined and integrated. The entire ship glowed a yellowish orange color.

"The crowd was gasping and people were mumbling, wondering what it could be. After hovering for a few minutes it slowly started to move, then began some incredible maneuvers. It made square turns with no radius and went up and down with the same precision. It moved faster and faster until it became difficult to follow and looked almost like a blur. This went on for almost ten minutes and everyone was spellbound.

"Finally, the craft slowly climbed to about 2,000 feet and hovered, then slowly disintegrated and a strange symbol appeared in its place. It was 600 feet square, glowed bright orange and lit up everything—the sky, the ground. Hovering below it were six flying saucers of different shapes illuminated by the symbol above them. Then the symbol and crafts disappeared and the show was over."

When he woke, he was excited and realized he might've seen a future event—the first official contact with extraterrestrials. He wonders when that will happen.

CHAPTER 9
EARTH 'SHAKINGS'

WARNINGS

Typically, abductees don't get much of an opportunity to ask Grays why they're here, but sometimes Grays and other aliens have addressed the matter. The messages that abductees bring back, either through what they consciously remember or through hypnotic regression, is often a warning related to coming Earth changes. In essence, depending on the source, either the aliens come to our assistance in a time of need or take advantage of our disabled condition, seize control or wipe out humanity.

On several different occasions during abductions in the 1970s through early 1990s, Diane Fine found herself in classroom settings on the craft. "Besides the medical technology I was shown, there were flat screen monitors, iPad-like devices with magnetic pens, 3-D modules that were used to monitor the Pacific Rim's volcanic activity, the ocean floor. When that technology actually started coming on the market, I was blown away."

Diane says these images depicting cataclysms, disasters, and planetary changes flashed past quickly. But the message was clear: the cataclysms were a result of humanity's disregard for the Earth. These apocalyptic environmental images have been reported by other researchers. In *Passport to the Cosmos, Human Transformation and Alien Encounters,* John Mack's last book on encounters, he wrote: "Indeed, it seems to me quite possible that the protection of the Earth's life is at the heart of the abduction phenomenon."

If we are to accept the experiences of abductees, what we are doing to Earth and what Earth is doing to us has been observed by intelligent beings from elsewhere. It seems that some are here to watch, others to help, and still others to take advantage of us for their own purposes. Those who want to help, though, may be bound by a code of ethics that prevents them from making direct contact.

NATIVE AMERICAN PROPHECIES

It could be that these Earth changes were foreseen in Native American prophecies that address a shift from one world to the next world. While the Hopis were not as precise in providing a date for the shift of worlds as the Mayans—whose calendar ended on December 21, 2012—their prophecy speaks of an approaching star and the return of a savior.

According to the prophecy, a blue star will appear in the sky. On that day the Blue Star Kachina will dance in the plaza and remove his mask, signifying the emergence of the Fifth World and a time of revelations. The Hopis call it the Day of Purification. Could it also be the Day of Disclosure? Could that blue star be a mother ship, possibly accompanied by other crafts?

Interestingly, Blue Star Kachina is also the Hopi name for the star system Sirius. The prophecy, as relayed by Hopi elders, also includes a foreboding message about great destruction on the planet. "The world shall rock to and fro. The white man will battle people in other lands—those who possessed the first light of wisdom. There will be many columns of smoke and fire such as the white man has made in the deserts not far from here."

The last sentence refers to nuclear testing in the desert of the Southwest in the 1950s, and the commentary seems to point to a nuclear attack on Arabic lands.

The prophecy continues: "Those who stay and live in the places of the Hopi shall be safe. Then there will be much to rebuild. And soon, very soon afterward, Pahana will return. He shall bring with him the dawn of the Fifth World. He shall plant the seeds of his wisdom in our hearts. Even now the seeds are being planted. These shall smooth the way to the Emergence into the Fifth World."

The Lakota (Sioux) Indians also believe that man has evolved through four ages, calling them the Age of Fire, Age of Rock, Age of the Bow, and Age of the Pipe. The Lakota prophecy suggests each age ends as man becomes a "two-heart"—infected with evil.

On the Hopi reservation is a boulder known as Prophecy Rock. It's etched with a symbolic message that includes three circles representing three 'world shakings.' According to the elders, the meaning of Prophecy Rock tells us that people of the Earth have forgotten that we are all related. As a result, the Creator wakes up the people by shaking the world.

Supposedly, the first two shakings have already occurred—World War I and World War II. The third is on the horizon, and in the aftermath Pahana will appear. Pahana had visited in the distant past and brought culture to the people and had promised to return. Even though he is often referred to as a 'white man', clearly he is enshrined with non-human qualities. With his reappearance linked to the appearance of a blue star in the sky, it's easy to theorize that Pahana was an advanced being from beyond Earth.

Here's a description of the legend, by Edmund Nequatewa from his book, *Truth of a Hopi*:

"...Pahana was wise and with his inventions had reached the rising sun and was coming back to them again, for they had seen the big eastern star and that was a sign and they were waiting for him. Every grandfather and grandmother...would tell their grandchildren to go out in the mornings before sunrise with sacred cornmeal to ask the sun to hurry the Pahana along so that he would come soon."

Of all the Native American cultures, the Mayans and their mysterious calendar have received the most attention. The ending of the calendar was widely misinterpreted as synonymous with the ending of the world. But for the Mayans, as other Native American cultures, the end of the Fourth World leads to the beginning of the Fifth World, a time of revival after massive changes.

Part of the mystique of the Maya culture relates to the speculation that they were visited by non-human entities from the stars and even that they might have been ruled by one such visitor. Kukulcan (known as Quetzalcoatl by the Aztecs) has been called a king and also a god. He supposedly arrived from elsewhere, similar to Pahana, and taught the Maya about agriculture, mathematics, medicine and astronomy.

While mainstream archaeologists reject the idea of an extraterrestrial influence, other researchers ask how else can we explain the Mayan calendar that can accurately predict lunar eclipses within 30 seconds? The Maya knew of planets that were not discovered until many centuries later, and accurately calculated the rotation of Venus. They may have been the first civilization to use the zero in mathematics.

Kukulcan was described by the Maya as appearing to be Caucasian, having blonde hair and blue eyes. While later kings who took the same name were warlike in nature, the original Kukulcan was benevolent and magical, a being with powers.

That description is similar to a type of tall, blond aliens who have been called 'Nordics.' Unlike the Grays, they are generally referred to as kind, helpful and concerned about human welfare. They have also been called 'space brothers' and Pleiadians, related to the star cluster the Pleiades.

ABDUCTEES AS PLANETARY EMPATHS

Some abductees believe that they have garnered new abilities as a result of their encounters. They experience frequent synchronicities, and are attuned to the planet, especially its violent upheavals—earthquakes, hurricanes, tsunamis, volcanic eruptions. They also frequently foresee human-made disasters, like 9-11. Typically, hours or days before a disaster, these individuals experience a variety of physical symptoms and discomforts—dizziness, nausea, fatigue or vertigo, anxiety without a known cause, breathlessness, chest or abdominal pains, or wildly fluctuating emotions, such as crying without known reason. In essence, they have become planetary empaths.

On March 11, 2011, at 2:46 p.m. Tokyo time, a 9.0 earthquake shook northern Japan for two minutes and shifted the planet on its axis by about nine inches. It was followed by a tsunami with thirty-foot waves that swept away entire villages, killed tens of thousands of people, and crippled the Fukushima Daiichi nuclear plant, resulting in a nuclear disaster classified as a Level 7, the same as Chernobyl.

By the end of 2012, the plant was still not functioning, the soil in the area was radioactive, mutant butterflies were being born, and the thousands who were evacuated due to high radioactivity in the area haven't returned to their homes. Radioactivity has been found in Pacific fish off the coast of the U.S. West Coast and debris from the disaster has washed up on coastal beaches.

It's estimated that it could take from ten to thirty years to completely dismantle and decommission the reactors. The Japanese government, the Tokyo Electric Power Company, and other authorities involved in the containment were caught by surprise.

But this triple disaster was no surprise to Diane Fine and Connie Cannon. They are both planetary empaths and believe the ability is a result of their abductions.

A week before the quake in Japan, Diane began to have severe physical symptoms she knew were related to an upcoming disaster. Her ears rang constantly, she suffered from extreme vertigo and excruciating migraines. She couldn't sleep, couldn't function, and ended up in the emergency room several times. A sense of profound sadness left her paralyzed.

Around the same time, Connie was in a grocery store one afternoon when she suddenly felt the ground shift violently beneath her and grabbed onto a shelf to keep her balance. Her head pounded, her vision blurred, nausea gripped her. She barely made it out of the store to her car. Her husband and the people around her didn't experience anything at all.

Four days before the triple disasters in Japan, Diane emailed us about her symptoms. She had severe ringing in her left ear, which for her is always a precursor to a quake or a volcanic eruption. Then other symptoms surfaced: severe vertigo, nausea, crippling fatigue. She has been experiencing these symptoms for more than twenty years, so she knows what to look for now.

"Although I was born intuitive and empathic, nothing prepared me for how those qualities would progress through life," Diane said. In the early 1990s, she began to notice that her intuitive flashes were expanding to include world events. The curious thing was how these flashes translated into physical symptoms. Occasionally, Diane's symptoms were accompanied by a dream or a vision, like watching a movie, but this wasn't the norm. Days before a world event she would feel a profound grief and heartache that nearly crippled her. She invariably wondered what was wrong with her.

"Then I began to notice a pattern. The grief episodes would precede an event—either a natural or man-made disaster—and disappear when the event happened: Princess Diana's death, the beginning of the Gulf war, the Columbine school shootings, the Virginia Tech shootings, the 2008 financial debacle. The pattern kept repeating."

One day before the Easter 2010 quake in Baja California, which caused the ground beneath Diane's home to move, her symptoms were so severe she couldn't get out of bed. The most worrisome symptom was that she was bleeding from the ears. She finally hauled herself out of bed and went to her doctor. But after a full exam, her physician couldn't offer any explanation. *We see the blood, but there doesn't seem to be a source,* she was told. *You don't have a brain tumor.*

Hardly comforting.

Before the horrific quake and tsunami in Sumatra, Indonesia in 2004, Diane and her husband were out running errands. Suddenly, her left ear had a long, sustained ringing and she experienced simultaneous visions of destruction and flooding. "I knew many would die. This was one of my first encounters with this type of visionary experience. I was disoriented and my husband had to hold me up until it was over. I told him what I was witnessing. I was horrified. I knew it would happen in three days, but didn't know *where* it would happen."

The night before the Indonesia quake and tsunami, Diane dreamed she was facing a goddess who was half-human, half-reindeer. She was a mixture of skin, fur and hair, had enormous antlers, and was very powerful. She was flinging Diane's body around like a lasso, holding her by the hair. When the creature shifted the orbit of Diane's body slightly, she suddenly knew the creature was Reindeer Woman.

At the time, Diane had no idea who Reindeer Woman was. But she did correlate her body in the dream with the Earth. Diane has a complex of autoimmune diseases and, long ago, came to believe that her body's illnesses were somehow directly linked to humanity's damage of the environment and that her condition was a mirror of a larger issue regarding the whole planet. So, in the dream, her body was the Earth. But who was this powerful goddess?

Days after the events in Sumatra, scientists announced that the earth's axis had shifted. The quake was the second strongest ever recorded and the Earth continued to oscillate for four months after the initial event. When Diane read about this shift of the Earth's axis, she realized that Reindeer Woman was somehow linked to the planet's axis.

"At the time, the only material I could find on reindeer goddesses was Linda Schierse Leonard's book *Creations Heartbeat: Following the Reindeer Spirit*. Leonard feels the reindeer is an excellent motif representing the re-emergence of the Goddess."

On February 24, 2010, Diane found a tattered novel on a shelf in a thrift store that caught her attention. Its cover featured a sketch of a rock with a pictograph of an antlered woman. She can't recall the title, but she handed the book to her husband and said: "The last time I saw reindeer woman, the Earth's axis shifted."

Her husband knew she was referring to the Sumatra quake and asked her if she wanted the book. Diane shook her head. She didn't feel well, the store was crowded, she needed to leave. Three days later, on February 27, 2010, Chile had an 8.8 earthquake off the coast of the Maule Region, with tsunami warnings issued for the Pacific Rim. Diane was stunned by the synchronicity of her dream, the tattered book, the Reindeer Woman motif, again.

On March 1, NASA's Jet Propulsion Laboratory in Pasadena, California, said that the 8.8-magnitude quake in Chile moved the Earth's axis by about 8 centimeters and shortened the day by 1.26 microseconds. Richard Gross, a geophysicist at the laboratory employed the same model that was used to estimate the effects of the 2004 Sumatran earthquake, which shifted the planet's axis by seven centimeters and shortened the day by 6.8 microseconds. Gross said the fact that the Chilean earthquake was in the Earth's mid-latitudes, instead of near the equator, meant it had shifted the axis further despite being smaller.

ENCOUNTERS AND PLANETARY EMPATHS

Some planetary empaths have had UFO encounters, sightings or dreams, but they don't believe they've ever been abducted.

For Natalie Thomas, a medium and mother of five in Queensland, Australia, symptoms start with a great sense of agitation that comes out of nowhere and "a dreadful sadness akin to grief or a broken heart." Most of the time when these feelings begin to surface, it's as if a switch has been flicked that allows her to feel the energy of events. The only thing she can equate it to is a sense of being "broken open."

That was how she felt shortly before the 6.3 quake in New Zealand on February 21, 2011. The emotional symptoms were accompanied by a profound fatigue, a buzzing and soreness in her ears and sore, itchy eyes.

Oddly enough, Vicki DeLaurentis, a mother and writer who lives on the other side of the planet from Natalie, experienced planetary symptoms before the New Zealand quake as well. On February 21, before the quake was widely reported outside New Zealand, her insomnia was extreme. "I kept waking up every hour, I was very emotional and I didn't know why." She now recognizes that when her tinnitus becomes really severe, a significant earthquake is happening somewhere.

Nancy Atkinson, a writer from Reno, Nevada, experienced some unusual symptoms two to three days before the Japanese quake: an electrical charge running up and down one of her legs. She also felt extremely sad. "I usually experience this when something really bad is happening somewhere."

For Jenean Gilstrap, a poet and artist from Shreveport, Louisiana, the most persistent symptoms before the Japan quake were heart palpitations and an unsteady gait that forced her to grab onto something to steady herself. "I felt like I was on a large ferry crossing turbulent waters in the local bay."

Before the earthquake in Haiti on January 12, 2010—a 7.7 followed by more than fifty aftershocks of 4.5 magnitude or greater—Jane Clifford, a psychic and healer in Wales, stopped abruptly in the middle of the living room and felt "a great upheaval of the earth, chaos and despair." Her entire body felt broken, crushed under heavy stones. She was also anxious and gloomy. The night before the quake in Japan in 2011, she sent us an email describing her symptoms: "I have the broken all over feeling again and a high pitched, clear ringing in my right ear."

The majority of planetary empaths with whom we've had contact are women. Since women are traditionally the nurturers in Western culture, this isn't surprising. There could be thousands of men who are planetary empaths, but men tend to talk less than women about their personal experiences, particularly of this nature.

Some of these planetary empaths have psychic or mediumistic abilities, and all have had experiences to one degree or another with UFOs. They are wives, mothers, and grandmothers who range in age from their twenties to their seventies. They work or have worked in a variety of professions— nursing, teaching, writing, alternative healing, computer programming, human resources. Several have chronic health issues but have learned to differentiate these health problems from the planetary empath symptoms. Connie and Diane, however, the two known abductees among these empaths, appear to have the most severe symptoms and are gradually learning to decode what their symptoms means.

Given the disaster images that abductees are so often shown, is it possible that planetary empaths represent an evolution in human consciousness? Is this ability something that might prove valuable in a world where disasters related to climate change become more numerous and frequent?

For some of these planetary empaths, vivid dreams or visions of a disaster are the first inkling that a natural or manmade disaster lies just ahead. On February 14, 2011, a full month before the triple catastrophes in Japan, Jenean Gilstrap and Nancy Atkinson's daughter, Jen, had parallel dreams about a tsunami in which they both saw entire towns being swept away.

Elena Stamataki, a 32-year-old woman from Greece, says that for nine or ten months before the disaster in Japan, she dreamed that she was in that country, in the aftermath of a tsunami, and was panicked and running with a child in her arms, trying to find a flight out of the country. In the dream, she knew something worse than the quake and tsunami were about to happen. That turned out to be the meltdown at Fukushima.

From April 25-28, 2011, the largest tornado outbreak ever recorded in the U.S. occurred. This outbreak set other records as well. It covered a broad swathe of the country, affecting Alabama, Arkansas, Georgia, Mississippi, Tennessee, and Virginia. It killed 348 people and four of the tornadoes were rated EF5, the highest ranking possible. On April 27, 2011 a record-breaking 205 tornadoes touched down. Entire towns were reduced to rubble.

Connie didn't have migraines associated with this tornado outbreak. Instead, she experienced a sensation that her head was too heavy for her neck to hold up. "I sometimes have right or left temporal headaches prior to these events. But the headaches come and go in waves and are always, like the ear noises, on one side or the other, never both, during a cluster of symptoms."

She believes the symptoms for the tornado outbreak were particularly severe because she grew up in Alabama, the state that was hit the worst. That personal connection increased her symptoms and their severity.

Nancy Atkinson's planetary empath symptoms always occur during an event, even if she hasn't heard about it yet, rather than before. "I think planetary empaths feel different things at different times. Empathic symptoms may well be linked to personal connections to a certain place. But I think these symptoms are also linked to *personal abilities*. My background in human resources means that human misery affects me."

Nancy's strongest empathic symptoms—particularly feelings of despair—occurred during the Rwanda massacre in 1994, when an estimated 800,000 people were killed. Over a period of a hundred days, about twenty percent of the Rwanda population was murdered, the culmination of ethnic tensions between the minority Tutsi, who had controlled the power for centuries, and the majority Hutu people. The movie, *Hotel Rwanda* was based on those events.

UNUSUAL SYMPTOMS AND SIGHTINGS

Nancy Atkinson has never been abducted, at least not to her knowledge. But when she was three months pregnant with her oldest daughter, Jen, she woke up one night to see flashing lights in the two small windows above her bed. She got up and went over to the large windows of her bedroom.

The entire area was lit up, as if under a brilliant full moon. She kept looking around and thinking, *Where's the moon?* There were no cars or other activity on the street below her window. "All of a sudden the baby in my stomach started spinning around and around. I looked down and could see my stomach moving!"

Her unborn daughter was doing somersaults. Before this time, the baby hadn't moved at all, which is normal. Fetal movement usually starts at around five months. Nancy was astounded and called out to her husband, Rich, so he could feel the spinning and see the lights. But he was sound asleep.

"I finally woke Rich and he said he didn't see or hear anything. I went back to bed but couldn't fall back to sleep. There was a small ranch with several cows a few streets over and I could hear the cows bawling until dawn. They were deeply frightened by something."

The next day, Nancy called everyone she knew in the area to find out what the lights might have been. She called the airport but they didn't have anything going on out of the ordinary. She called the city's mosquito control, but they didn't have any equipment in her area. She called the street-cleaning people. "I called literally everyone I knew of that could possibly use flashing lights. I never found any explanation. My daughter didn't move again until around the fifth month—right when the expectancy book said she would."

Interestingly, her daughter has experienced a vast array of experiences related to nonhuman entities and poltergeist phenomenon. She also considers herself a planetary empathy. In early 2011, Trish and some other women maintained a private blog to share their psychic and empathic experiences. Two days before the quake in Japan, Jen reported "a buffet of paranormal experiences."

She heard inexplicable *whooshing* sounds that were coming from outside her home. They pulsed louder, softer, came and went. She woke up her husband and made him listen to the sounds, but he didn't have any idea what they might be. She actually looked outside, half expecting to see a giant UFO, but didn't see anything. Her bed vibrated for no apparent reason off and on throughout the night, and she felt as if "the top of my head was opening up and information was being taken out and other stuff put in. It freaked me out, but a very loud voice said, *Do not be afraid*. So I remained cautiously observant."

At around this same time, her young son had a night terror where he was yelling, "*No, no, I don't want to go with those guys.* Yet, he was able to carry on a conversation with her at the same time.

Diane also experienced poltergeist phenomenon before the events in Japan. On March 8, three days before the quake, she wrote about two poltergeist experiences—loud stomping and sounds like a door slamming shut, but with no apparent physical source. These experiences were accompanied by an epic migraine, the worst she'd ever had.

After we posted on our blog about planetary empaths, Anne N wrote us. She said that until she had read the post, she thought she might be a hypochondriac or crazy because she experienced many of the same symptoms before planetary disasters.

Intrigued, we asked if she'd ever had any UFO encounters or had been abducted. As far as she knows, she has never been abducted, she replied, but has been seeing UFOs off and on since she was eight.

"I have seen different kinds, doing different things. A few look like equilateral planes. Others like spheres. One strange thing I saw three years ago looked similar to a big brown straight stick that crossed over the roofs of buildings, clearing them by about ten feet, then it disappeared from sight. The sudden disappearance of this thing surprised me. First it was there, then it wasn't."

Jenean Gilstrap isn't an abductee, either. But she has experienced several encounters, which could relate to her apparent ability to detect disasters before they happen. One of her most vivid and personal encounters occurred in late May or early June 1969, when she and her children were traveling by bus from Little Rock to Monroe, in northeastern Louisiana. The bus was full, so they had to share seats. Her son, five at the time, was sitting next to the window. On a rural stretch of road between Sterlington and Monroe, which are about fifteen miles apart, her son tugged on her arm, drawing her attention to the window.

It was broad daylight and when Jenean looked up, she saw a huge UFO in the sky over the fields on her side of the bus. "I was so startled that I closed my eyes and then reopened them to make sure I was really seeing what I knew I was seeing. Sure enough, the UFO was still there and the other passengers on that side of the bus were all looking at it, talking about it. Passengers on the other side of the bus got out of their seats and crowded into the aisle to see it better."

By then, there was a lot of commotion and a barely subdued panic as people urged the driver to drive faster. Some shouted that they wanted off the bus, others were spellbound, and everyone jockeyed for a better look. *Oh my God, what is that thing?* All the while, Jenean and her kids watched it, fascinated. The craft moved slowly, parallel to the bus and low enough in the sky so that Jenean could see it out the window without straining to look upward. It was close enough for her to see the textured surface.

She remembers trying to memorize all the details of the craft—its size, shape, color, how it moved. It made no sound, no engines or wings were visible. Nothing about it was characteristic of a plane. Jenean recalls it was at least the size of a football field, and was oval or circular, with a transparent domed top. "The dome seemed clear, but I don't remember being able to see through it. There was a row of what appeared to be windows or lights encircling the bottom of the dome. The object's body was gray, like a battleship, and not shiny. I remember there seemed to be a texture or mottling to the matte finish, like old cast iron cookware."

The UFO continued moving alongside the bus for quite a distance, more than just a few minutes. Then, just as suddenly as it had appeared, it made a 45-degree turn to the right, tore upward, and was instantly and completely out of sight. "It literally zoomed away without making a sound. The bus was now speeding as the driver attempted to outrun it to the next town. Passengers were hysterical."

When the bus pulled into the Monroe station, news reporters were already there. Jenean didn't have any idea how they'd heard about the UFO, but suddenly felt fearful about the experience, as if *they* were looking for *her*. All she wanted to do was get away from the station with her kids. She felt so overwhelmed with fear that she left the station without even gathering up their luggage.

She and her kids took a taxi to Jenean's mother's house, but even then, her fear didn't subside. She desperately wanted to flee—literally—to somewhere she and her children couldn't be found. "To this day, I am unsure of my profound reaction. I grew up having seen UFOs in my family's many travels. UFOs were discussed by my parents, they were nothing new to me. Until that bus trip, I'd never responded with anything but total curiosity before. This experience was my first up close and personal encounter. There was absolutely *no* doubt what this object was, let alone what it was not. It was daytime, clear."

Not long after she arrived at her mother's, reporters and law enforcement personnel called the house. Several days later, three men came to her mother's house to interview Jenean about what had happened on the bus. "They were—I kid you not—dressed completely in black and identified themselves as military personnel from Wright-Patterson Air Force Base. I told them what I had seen and when they asked me sketch the object, I did so. They took it with them. At least one of the men gave me a business card when I asked for it. Some time later, when I phoned the number on the card, there was no such number. I called the base directly, but no one had heard of the person for whom I asked."

Interestingly, some of the news reports identified this UFO—seen by a busload of people—as a smoke cloud emanating from an industrial site in Sterlington.

When Jenean was writing up this encounter for us, she experienced an odd synchronicity that captured her attention. Her phone rang and the ID indicated the call was from Ohio. "We don't know anyone in Ohio. But it's where Wright-Patterson Air Force Base is located. When I answered the phone, no one was there."

Wright-Patterson in Dayton, Ohio conducts research and development of new weaponry, tests new weapons technology, and is the home to the Air Force Institute of Technology. It also houses the U.S. Air Force's National Air and Space Intelligence Center. During the Cold War, reverse engineering of foreign government aircraft was undertaken at the base. Even more pertinent to Jenean's experience, however, is the base's connection to UFO lore.

Project Blue Book, the Air Force's *official* investigation of the UFO phenomenon (1947-1969), was headquartered at Wright-Patterson. According to UFO researchers and theorists, this base, along with the Groom Lake/Area 51 installation in Nevada, is where wreckage of the Roswell UFO crash was shipped via a B-29. The material at Wright-Patterson was allegedly placed in Hangar 18.

Jenean's encounter was remarkable in that it took place during daylight hours, at close range, in full view of a busload of people who watched the large craft for ten or fifteen minutes. Cells phones and social media didn't exist then, yet the news media was waiting at the Monroe station when the bus pulled in. With dozens of witnesses, this kind of encounter is difficult to cover up. But cover ups have happened time and again.

These encounters often take place in the darkness, on lonely roads. The norm is isolation, a light or lights in the sky, confusion, missing time, gaps in memory. The norm is like the encounter Charles had. Or what Betty and Barney Hill experienced. Or like Connie and her son's experience on Warner-Robbins Air Force Base. The usual circumstances of an encounter or abduction, whether it occurs in darkness or in daylight, force you to question whether you're actually experiencing what you think you are.

As Diane Fine so aptly put it, "This phenomenon is so tricky. It's so hard to know what to do or what you feel when your mind and perceptions are being messed with."

CHAPTER 10
IDENTIFYING FLYING OBJECTS

MASS SIGHTINGS

Technology has made it possible for anyone who sees a UFO to capture it on video and upload it to You Tube, Twitter, Facebook and every other social media outlet. Combined with witness testimonies over the decades, we now know that UFOs apparently come in an array of shapes and sizes.

They are shaped like ovals, cigars, triangles, trapezoids, disks, spheres, coins flipped on their sides, boomerangs, crescents, hexagons, Vs, lenticulars, diamonds. They are black, silver, metallic, smooth, textured, and can change colors and shapes. They range in sizes as huge as a football stadium and as small as a VW. The crafts reportedly move at incredible speeds, can hover, hang seemingly motionless in the sky, and are capable of astounding maneuvers. They usually make no sound, don't have wings, often have a dome on top, and even lit portholes.

Typically, they don't look like weather balloons, birds, or smoke emanating from industrial sites. They don't look like the planet Venus, a meteor or comet or fireball. In sightings where there are hundreds of witnesses, officials often scramble to find a "suitable" explanation.

On March 13, 1997, around 7 p.m., the first report of a sighting that would later be called The Phoenix Lights came in from Henderson, Nevada. The sighting was followed by others over Kingman, Arizona, southeast to Prescott, on to Phoenix, and then as far south as Tucson. A tremendous, slow-moving craft was seen by thousands of witnesses, who said that when the object passed overhead, it blotted out the stars. As John Alexander noted in *UFOs: Myths, Conspiracies and Realities*, this detail "means the UFO was a solid object and could not possibly be light aircraft flying in formation as some have alleged."

In the Phoenix area, between 8 and 9 p.m., there were two key sightings in which witnesses reported seeing an object with six points of light, a second object with eight points of light, and a ninth object that moved in unison with the second object. The shapes of these objects varied from triangles to Vs to disks.

A truck driver on I-17, who was headed to a plant near Luke Air Force base, claimed that for two hours, a pair of amber-colored UFOs moved along ahead of him, southward. When he arrived at the plant, the UFOs hovered nearby and the driver climbed to a higher elevation to get a better look at them. He said three F-16s blasted out of the air force base and aimed straight for the UFOs, which instantly disappeared.

When questioned, the air force claimed the lights were flares dropped by A-10 Warhog aircraft involved in a training exercise. But it took them four months to explain the flare theory and their timing was off: the flares were dropped after 10 p.m. But by then, the facts didn't matter. The skeptics announced the case was closed.

Three months after the sightings, in June 1997, then governor Fyfe Symington held a press conference with one of his aides, who wore a space alien costume. The whole press conference was intended to demean the sightings. Yet, ten years later, when Symington was no longer governor, he admitted that he'd seen what other witnesses had reported, a huge V-shaped craft that had blocked out the stars. He talked about it publicly on national TV and said, "As a pilot and former Air Force officer, I can definitively say that this craft did not resemble any man-made objects I'd ever seen."

Unfortunately, his public confession came ten years too late. The disinformation and ridicule had worked. The sightings were dismissed or ignored by the mainstream media.

Numerous mass sightings have occurred over the years and *National Geographic* has documented the top ten, which date back to 1853. In the 20th and 21st century, these mass sightings include: the Kecksburg Incident on December 9, 1965; the V-shaped lights over the Hudson Valley on March 24, 1983; the UFO on the New Jersey Turnpike on July 24; and the Stephenville Lights on January 8, 2008. To this list, we would add the Gulf Breeze, Florida sightings that occurred in 1997. Google any of them. The sightings and how authorities dealt with them are fascinating and provide insight about the lengths to which the government or debunkers go to deny and cover up.

A more recent case occurred at an air show in Chile in 2010 in which an unknown object literally darted around approaching jets flying in formation. Seven videos taken on cameras and cell phones recorded the object from different angles and points of observation. Yet, skeptics dismissed the object as a bug, possibly a beetle, passing in front of the camera. But how could bugs account for the same object that was spotted on seven cameras?

Possibly, the UFO appeared at an air show near a formation of jets as a means of intentionally exposing the unidentified craft to multiple cameras. Such mass sightings can't be easily dismissed by anyone without a strong bias, especially when they are filmed by multiple sources. They instantly shatter—and broaden—worldviews and open us to the idea that reality is far more complex than we think. The more frequently such exhibitions are recorded, the more open people become to the reality that UFOs are among us.

A personal encounter like Charles Fontaine experienced can do the same thing, of course, but when you're the only one who has experienced the encounter or seen the UFO, you may feel, like Charles did, that you've lost your mind. Fortunately, for Charles, his wife also witnessed the mysterious cones of light and experienced some of the same after-effects.

Then there are sightings by individuals who already believe that UFOs exist, who may have had sightings in the past, and whose experiences provide significant information about these crafts.

UP CLOSE AND PERSONAL

On September 8, 2010, Jenean Gilstrap woke suddenly at 3:30 a.m. and couldn't fall back asleep. She tossed and turned awhile and lay there, staring out her window. It faced west and wasn't covered by blinds or curtains. She finally rolled onto her side, picked up the remote control and turned on her TV. When she looked out again, a massive craft filled her window.

It flew low, silently. Jenean was so startled, she thought she was dreaming. For a reality check, she looked to see if the TV had come on. It had, so she knew she was awake. She glanced back at the window and couldn't take her eyes off the craft.

"It came toward the house, directly from the west, moving straight toward and over our house, headed east, and kept flying low. I was seeing it from underneath, while sitting on my bed, peering upward through the top part of my windows. It moved so slowly that I wondered if it was going to crash. I couldn't understand how something so colossal could stay in the air, so close to the ground."

The silent craft had three front lights that were bright, a pure white, but they weren't beams. Jenean sat there, entranced, her mind churning out endless questions: Was it a law enforcement sort of thing? Was there a beam somewhere following a fugitive on the ground? "I knew it wasn't anything I've ever seen before—ever. It was just like scenes from *Independence Day*, watching this craft move above me, seeing only the underside of it as it approached."

Jenean described the shape as two overlaid triangles with curved corners. All the lights on the craft were the same size, except the center light on the bottom, which was large. The body was dark black, but on the six convex sections, three on each side, there was a lighter color, a matte-like dark gray color. These sections had no lights but the lights from the points and the center light were bright enough to render the convex sections visible.

"As it came closer, I kept telling myself mentally to wake my daughter. I wanted her to see it. I wanted to follow the craft visually through her east-facing bedroom windows. But I was totally mesmerized and couldn't get up. I felt immobilized. I kept thinking I needed to take a picture with my phone or something, but I was afraid that if I looked away, it would go away. So I sat there and tried to memorize every single detail."

The craft continued to move slowly toward Jenean's house and finally, over the top of it. "Then it was gone from view and I just kept sitting there. Then I remember wondering what had just happened."

Oddly, she didn't remember to tell her daughter about it the next morning. "Why I didn't remember such an incident is beyond me. It's unusual for me *not* to remember, *not* to have written it down."

Memory lapses, confusion, and feeling of immobilization or paralysis are common with encounters. As Diane Fine says, "I have had the same thing happen to me while experiencing various phenomenon. There is definitely something that happens during these encounters that seems to override our own will and stops us from doing what we want."

In 2010, when we wrote about Jenean's experience on our blog, the post received more than a hundred comments. One of the commenters was a diehard skeptic and a frequent contributor on a blog maintained by professional skeptic James Randi. When Randi was given the MacArthur award back in the late 1980s, it gave him a cache he probably wouldn't have had otherwise and this particular skeptic was one of his avid acolytes-smart, well informed, and malicious. He's also a computer hacker and used his skills against us, taking over our blog, changing passwords, and even posted an apology to himself that was supposedly from Rob.

This incident drove home just how spiteful some skeptics can be when their worldview is threatened. It's why many experiencers remain mum and why researchers risk their reputations when they explore this area. Mainstream science says UFOs do not exist, that when they are allegedly sighted, witnesses are actually seeing something mundane. Governments, for the most part, are either mum on the question of UFOs or dismissive.

However, with the advent of smart phones and social media new avenues have opened for recording and disseminating images of mysterious objects to large numbers of people. While it may be difficult at times to sort out the fakes from genuine UFOs, the availability and abundance of videos and images and the forums for discussing them hopefully will move us closer to answers.

INSIDE THE CRAFT

In the winter of 2012, Trish was interviewed for a segment of William Shatner's *Weird or What?* in Toronto on the subject of mind control. She was asked to talk about Wolfgang Pauli, the theoretical physicist who won a Nobel in 1945 for his exclusion principle and also collaborated with Carl Jung on synchronicity.

Specifically, she was there to talk about the 'Pauli effect,' the spontaneous breakdown of laboratory equipment in his presence. This seemingly psychokinetic effect was to be presented as a possible theory for what was happening to a woman who believed she was the victim of government mind control.

Trish's segment was filmed separately, so we had no idea at the time of the interview that much of the show would be about alien abductions and mind control. We found that out months later when we watched the episode. By then we were involved in the writing of this book. So, for us, watching it was a startling synchronicity.

Yet, we both recalled talking to the producer briefly about UFOs during a break in the filming. The topic came up when we mentioned that Rob had been interviewed about the Bermuda Triangle for an episode of the History Channel's *UFO Hunter*. The producer admitted he was skeptical about the reality of UFOs. "Where are the photos? Where are the videos?"

His comment surprised us. There's an abundance of video and photos of UFOs and testimonies about what these crafts look like. A Google search of the term UFO videos turned up 15,400,000 hits. The real issue is whether or not the videos are real, and what the videos show us. Some of this material is compelling and some of it, well, not so much. Possibly the producer was referring to close-up photos or video of crafts *and* aliens. In that sense, he is right. So far, there have only been vague and highly questionable photos of aliens.

Likewise, there are no known photos or videos of the inside of these crafts. So what we know about the interior comes from the abductees themselves. Mack, Hopkins, Jacobs and other researchers have included such information in their books, and the descriptions Connie and Diane provide certainly fall right in line with their findings.

During one abduction experience, Connie and her son found themselves in an enormous craft. The interior was multi-sided, like an octagon, but with eighteen or twenty internal sections. "These sections had gurneys, tables, stretchers in them like an emergency room, but there were no curtains or anything separating one from another," Connie said. "Some of these tables had humans on them, some of the humans were clothed, some were completely naked. Grays were doing something to the humans, I don't know what. There were Grays everywhere."

Connie and her son were rushing and racing around, desperately seeking some kind of exit, but there wasn't one. It was somehow transmitted to them that the Grays were *trying to change their identities* and that the change had already begun. The Gray chasing them was clumsy, unable to catch them.

"On one very large part of the 'circle', directly across the area from the stretchers, there was what appeared to be a huge control board or system that went from the floor to the ceiling of the craft. It looked like computers and other types of high tech equipment, all with flashing lights in colors, and buttons and levers and switches."

Seated at the console was a former NASA ground astronaut Connie knew—Clark McClelland. Even though Connie had never met him in person, he had contacted her some years earlier, through a mutual friend, about editing a book he'd written. The project hadn't worked out, but over a period of several years they had communicated through email and by phone. He was able to rotate the chair in which he was seated and look at Connie and her son. He told her that neither she nor her son would be hurt as long as he was onboard.

The chair in which McClelland sat was something Connie had seen before, during an earlier abduction where she was strapped into a rotating chair with a restraint similar to a seatbelt, except that she couldn't release it on her own. In that abduction (described in chapter 4), the bottom of the craft had slid open and an infrared light, or something like it, allowed her to see inside houses.

She has no memory of leaving the craft during this experience. The next morning when she woke up, she felt dizzy, nauseated, disoriented. She immediately emailed Clarke and told him she and her son had been on board a spacecraft with him during the night. That was all Connie said. She didn't provide any other details.

In response, McClelland proceeded to tell *her* about the encounter, about what he had said, and what "*they* were trying to do to us, the identity switch. "He *had* to have been there or he wouldn't possibly have known those things. I got absolutely furious because he refused to tell me anything else; he wouldn't answer my questions. He said he wasn't allowed."

With one exception, Connie has never known how she was taken aboard the crafts. The exception happened in 1949, when she was just seven, and the memory is vivid for her. "An entity had me tucked under its arm and we were gliding up what looked like a beam of light of some kind. Remember, there was no such thing way back then as *beam me up Scottie*. The entity that was holding me under its arm, carrying me up this slanted beam, was strangely shaped—not a Gray. There was a high-frequency *humming* sound that even now freaks me out when I hear anything like it."

She didn't actually see the entity taking her into the craft, it simply carried her into this peculiar beam that was wide at its bottom and grew narrower as they went up. "We glided. The entity wasn't walking. It was moving like we would move on an escalator—something I had never seen or been on in 1949."

Diane Fine's memories about the inside of the craft are similar to Connie's in terms of the size. Diane, like Connie, saw humans lying on operating tables. Some of them were unconscious, others were awake, but not moving. She sensed these humans were like her, living people, abductees from Earth.

"Sometimes I was in a large space with diffused light and some kind of fog that prevented me from seeing exactly where I was," Diane said. It frustrated and angered her. Horrifying enough that she had been taken against her will. But to be prevented from *seeing* the full details of her location was equally terrifying. It made her feel even more powerless. But perhaps that was the point.

Other researchers have noted this phenomenon as well. An abductee named Ed with whom John Mack worked described under hypnosis how his vision was limited in some way and it angered him. "I hate being in this position of no control," he told Mack in *Abduction*. "I hate this! Damn it!"

During one abduction, Diane found herself in a room that was similar to a Navy ship command room, but much nicer. There was a group of beings—not Grays, many of them were human-looking. The beings appeared to be a team, preparing for a mission, and were gathered around a striking being that was about four feet tall, hairy all over, and dressed in red and orange robes. "He was held in high esteem for his wisdom and was about to travel to a planet—not Earth- to accomplish something important. I could see outer space outside the window, brilliant stars against the blackness."

What sets these experiences apart from those of many abductees is that Connie and Diane didn't undergo hypnosis to retrieve these memories. Both women have remembered their experiences consciously or through dreams or while meditating.

The one time Connie tried hypnosis—to retrieve the specifics of the threat made when she and her son were abducted to Warner-Robins—she bolted out of it, screaming. The block on that memory is apparently too strong to break through. Thanks to techniques that Diane learned from a Tibetan Lama under whom she studied, she has been able to remember most of her abductions.

In spite of the certainty both women maintain about what happened to them, they are well aware that mainstream science rejects their claims. From the perspective of the current scientific paradigm, there are no aliens here, except in our imaginations, so there are no alien abductions. In the next chapter, we look at alternative explanations that scientists have offered.

CHAPTER 11
SKEPTICS AND DISBELIEVERS

A cross cultures and across time people have recounted mysterious encounters with supernatural entities that abduct humans. The beings, fairies and the djinn among them, enter our physical world from other dimensions and provide us with magical abilities to see the future or heal the sick. But they also take something from us, a physical part of us that they move into their non-physical reality.

When such ancient supernatural forces appear in the modern world in the form of alien abductions, they collide with science, the media and technology—the gods of our time. Those who speak out about their encounters are typically ridiculed and derided.

Bad enough that these experiences are so bewildering and terrifying to the individuals affected that many avoid confiding in family members. But if their stories leak out to a wider audience, they fear being scorned, shunned by friends, family and neighbors, and possibly even losing their jobs.

Unfortunately, ridicule is a powerful weapon. Just ask former U.S. Congressman Dennis Kucinich, who admitted to a UFO sighting. During the Democratic primary debates in 2007, the late Tim Russert of NBC asked Kucinich about his interest in UFOs. "Shirley MacLaine writes in her new book that you sighted a UFO over her home in Washington state, that you found the encounter extremely moving, that it was a triangular craft, silent and hovering, that you felt a connection to your heart and heard directions in your mind. Now, did you see a UFO?"

"Uh, I did. It was an unidentified flying object, OK? It's like, it's unidentified. I saw something." Kucinich went on to joke about moving his campaign office to Roswell, New Mexico, and suggested that more people in this country have seen UFOs than approve of George Bush.

His sighting became fodder for ridicule in March 2010 when he announced he would support President Obama's health care reform bill.

Rush Limbaugh, never one to mince words, said, "They either threatened him with a UFO trip, or they offered to make sure that in his case his preexisting condition of mental illness will not be a barrier of any kind of coverage that he gets down the road."

Many people who have seen unidentified flying objects don't report them for a variety of reasons. They don't want to get involved or face possible ridicule. It's not worth the hassle. Or, they don't know where to report a sighting. They might also begin to doubt the validity of what they saw and assume that it was something ordinary. The stakes, of course, rise dramatically for anyone who reports close contact with a craft and its crew, or an abduction.

Adding to the problem is the view of some scientists who say that so-called abductees are scientifically illiterate, logically impaired. According to those scientists, when so-called abductees are hypnotized, they imagine events that never happened and are incapable of distinguishing external reality from fantasies.

But that description doesn't fit Charles and Helene Fontaine, Connie Cannon, Diane Fine, or Bruce Gernon—the people whose dramatic stories are the focus of this book. All are educated, understand the scientific method, are relentlessly curious, always looking for answers to better understand what happened to them. None of their stories were derived from hypnosis.

AN ASTONISHING SURVEY

The highly regarded Roper Organization conducted a survey of 6,000 Americans to find out how many had been abducted by aliens. Surprisingly, two percent of Americans fit the abductee profile. That's one out of every 50 people, or 33 million Americans. In addition, an unexpected number of the people who fit the abductee profile were categorized as 'influentials.' That group includes adults, ages 35 to 45, who have higher than average incomes and hold positions of political or social authority. They are trend-setters, defining morality and public policy. They lead rather than follow.

The results of the 2003 survey baffled the Roper Organization, which expected nothing of the sort. The report was published and confidentially distributed to every member of The American Psychiatric Association. We came across it while perusing declassified government documents related to UFOs that are available at theblackvault.com.

Skeptics, however, say that if that many Americans were being abducted, there would be more evidence of it, more witnesses. It would be common knowledge, a serious law enforcement issue and a national security problem. However, if the abductions are conducted by advanced beings with superior abilities and technology, then it's feasible that their covert activities could easily escape detection. That would be especially true if the government and military were discreetly involved in a secret program of cooperation.

WHAT SCIENTISTS SAY

Theories abound by mainstream scientists and researchers about people who claim alien contact. Some of the explanations offered by skeptics actually seem as bizarre as the abductions themselves. One researcher suggests that alien abductees are experiencing lucid dreams triggered by media attention on UFOs and related abductions. In other words, it's all a dream, regardless of how real it seems.

The problem with that theory is that many abductees are awake when abductions occur and don't find themselves in bed when it's over. Some abductions involve more than one person, as in the case of Charles and Helene, and both recall the incident. So were they both dreaming the same thing even though they were sure they were awake and standing on the back porch? Connie was driving a car and one of her sons accompanied her. Diane was with three friends and had stopped at a bar-restaurant.

Other explanations for alien encounters include psychological conditions such as fantasy-prone personalities, repression of abuse, and hysterical contagion—*others have been abducted so that's what happened to me*. Psychiatric explanations include psychosis, multiple personality disorder, and temporal lobe dysfunction. However, extensive research has shown that people who claim to have had encounters with aliens are no more psychotic than the general population.

However, the singular explanation for abduction scenarios that is overwhelmingly preferred by skeptics is the influence of hypnosis. Interestingly, only two of our subjects have tried hypnotic regression and in both cases the process was unsuccessful. Charles was never able to enter a hypnotic state and Connie started screaming as she entered one and the session was ended.

Yet, since hypnosis is a commonplace technique for obtaining details of abductions, it's worth taking a closer look at the procedure.

HYPNOTIC REGRESSIONS

Skeptics typically work from the fundamental concept that abductions are delusions with no external reality. Susan Clancy, author of *Abducted: How People Come to Believe They Were Abducted by Aliens* (published by Harvard University Press), went a step beyond that. As a Harvard PhD candidate when she began her study of abductions, her premise was that abductions can't be real because aliens don't exist.

Clancy took up the study of alien abductions essentially as an afterthought. She readily admits she had no interest in the subject. However, she had studied hypnosis and found herself at the center of a controversy regarding memories that women have of sexual abuse. In her research, Clancy contended that women who were hypnotically regressed to supposed blocked memories of childhood sexual abuse were prone to creating false memories. As a result, she found herself being seen as a 'secret enemy' of those who had shared their painful memories with her. "But then a safer way to study the reaction of false memories turned up," she wrote.

And that safer way was—you guessed it—to research alien abductions.

Harvard had just finished its 14-month investigation of John Mack's work with abductees and an opportunity arose for Clancy to study abductees in a laboratory environment. The intent, Clancy wrote in her book, was to answer this question: "Did they react to scary abduction memories the same way they reacted to scary events that had actually happened?"

In other words, from the onset, the premise was to assume that no one had been abducted by aliens, that the memories were false. "Here was a group that had 'repressed memories,' but the memories would be much less painful to hear about than memories of childhood sexual abuse. Even better, alien abductees were people who had developed memories of a traumatic event that I could be fairly certain had never occurred."

One scientist and UFO researcher who read Clancy's book, commented: "It is hard to imagine so-called research starting out with such strong bias. Is this what passes for research at Harvard University?"

Clancy thinks that memories of alien abductions are imposed by biased hypnotists through their leading questions. But David Jacobs, author of *The Threat* and other books on alien abductions, thinks that the main problem with hypnotic regressions of abductees is that naïve hypnotists aren't able to distinguish actual events recalled from fantasies and screen memories. Unlike Clancy, he accepts the possibility that abductees encounter alien beings. However, he doesn't assume that the story told by the abductee is accurate. Some hypnotists, Jacobs says, accept an abductee's story too easily and proceed to ask leading questions that reinforce what might be a fantasy or a screen memory imposed by the alien abductor. "The abductee has unconsciously led the hypnotist and the hypnotist has reciprocated by unwittingly validating the abductee," Jacobs writes.

He uses the hypothetical example of an abductee under hypnosis who says that he was playing a game similar to Monopoly with the aliens while aboard the ship. But the street names on the game were strange. Jacobs suggests that an inexperienced hypnotist might take the bait and ask for the names. That would lead to more fantasy.

Jacobs noted that in his years of investigating abductions, he has never heard of anyone playing board games. Therefore, he would question the abductee about the circumstances surrounding the event rather than delving into questions about the game itself.

"Because I know that people will sometimes confabulate, especially in the first few hypnotic sessions, I would immediately suspect in this case that confabulation was at work—although I must always remember that it is possible that aliens *did* play Monopoly with the abductee."

He would ask the abductee to describe the sequence of events and move him forward and back in time. He would also ask what the aliens were doing. Were they standing or sitting? Where were they looking and what were they looking at? "In other words, I would search for the alien visualization procedures that might have instilled this image in the abductee's mind."

Jacobs says such screen memories are put in place so that the abductee doesn't readily recall what really happened to him. In other cases, an abductee might slip into a dissociative state in which he confuses internal fantasies with external events. Uncritical hypnotists, he says, add to the confusion about alien abductions. "By uncritically accepting (and not challenging), by naively assuming that what is sincerely told is correct, and by defending this as 'reality,' inexperienced and naïve researchers muddy the waters for competent investigators, allow people to think that events have happened to them that have not, and add to the incredulity of the general public."

While Jacobs is tough on non-skeptical hypnotists, he's also convinced that alien abductions are real. Clancy, on the other hand, thinks they are all fantasies or screen memories stimulated by the hypnotist. She leaves no room for the existence of aliens, much less those who abduct humans. She wrote: "The whole idea of aliens coming to earth in UFOs and kidnapping humans for medical and genetic experimentation is not only extremely unlikely—it's downright silly."

Clancy grants that abductees probably aren't psychotic, but "they hold false beliefs—ones that appear to be natural by-products of their attempts to explain the unusual things that have happened to them."

She also contends that disbelievers need not worry about being abducted during the night. "I can say with great confidence that if you're not a believer already (at least to some extent), you're not going to acquire memories of alien abduction. No one goes to bed totally uninterested in aliens and wakes up screaming, "Oh my God, I was just abducted by aliens!"

Clancy should talk to Charles and Helene Fontaine. They went to bed one night completely uninterested in aliens and UFOs. Their encounter occurred in the morning after they got up. Clancy has no explanation for waking abductions, when most of them take place, or abductions involving more than one person. She also has no explanation for people who recall their UFO encounters without the use of hypnosis.

Clancy is a true *disbeliever*. Jacobs is skeptical about the stories told by hypnotized abductees, but is convinced that aliens are here and abducting people. A continent separates these beliefs. Clancy, it seems, can get away with questionable research and a strong bias because her arguments are favored by mainstream scientists, who tend to look away when the subject of UFOs and abductions surfaces.

Stanton Friedman, a physicist and UFO researcher, wrote that he was shocked by how much bias and prejudice Clancy revealed in her book. "She should have been flunked for her gross inaccuracy in her accounts, brief though they were, of various cases about which I am well informed. Remember that her so-called research was conducted at Harvard University using government research grants and the book was published by Harvard University Press. I guess they couldn't afford a fact checker."

Friedman goes on to say: "What is really crazy here, to me as a scientist, is that normally one expects somebody beginning research in a new area to do a literature search first. She couldn't be bothered."

THE SCIENCE DILEMMA

In 2012, the National Geographic Channel commissioned a poll by Kelton Research, a market research company, to find out how many people in the U.S believe that UFOs are real. It was done to promote their new TV series,

Chasing UFOs. The intriguing results?

Thirty-six percent of respondents believe UFOs exist. Given the current population of the U.S. in the fall of 2012, that's about 112 million people. Nearly four out of five Americans think the U.S. government has kept information about UFOs secrets from the public. The study showed that 77 percent of Americans believe there are signs that aliens have visited Earth, and one in 10 respondents claim to have personally witnessed an alien spaceship. More than half—55 percent—believe there are real MIBs who threaten people who have had sightings.

But statistics like these don't impress scientists. Paul Davies, author of *The Eerie Science: Renewing Our Search for Alien Intelligence,* seems to echo the earlier skeptics of falling rocks when he refers to atmospheric conditions as one explanation for UFO sightings.

Davies wrote that "the vast majority of them get explained straightforwardly as weird atmospheric effects, aircraft seen under unusual conditions, bright planets, etc....So it's tempting to conclude that if 95 percent of sightings can be explained without too much effort, then so could the remaining 5 per cent if we had enough information at our disposal, because there is nothing to elevate that residue from the rest, apart from being more puzzling."

But some scientists are willing to challenge the scientific orthodoxy. In *Science Set Free,* author and biologist Rupert Sheldrake argues that the current scientific worldview is entrenched in nineteenth century assumptions about the nature of reality. He wasn't referring specifically to UFOs, but what Sheldrake says certainly applies to the way most scientists regard the question of UFOs.

These long-held assumptions, Sheldrake said, have "hardened into dogmas" and are constricting scientific progress. In this worldview, materialism is king. "Contemporary science is based on the claim that all reality is material or physical. There is no reality but material reality. Consciousness is a by-product of the physical activity of the brain. Matter is unconscious. Evolution is purposeless. The laws of nature are fixed... Unexplained phenomena such as telepathy are illusory."

These dogmas make it easy for science to dismiss UFO sightings and encounters as nothing more than a fantasy the brain spins, colorful fiction. With mass sightings, like with the Phoenix Lights, that kind of dismissal is a bit more challenging. But once the air force provided an explanation—flares—scientists didn't have to bother explaining it away.

One of the biggest UFO flaps occurred between July 12-29, 1952, when a series of UFO sightings took place over Washington, D.C. The most publicized sightings occurred on consecutive weekends, July 19-20 and July 26-27, and prompted President Harry Truman to personally call Captain Edward J. Ruppelt, supervisor of the air force's Project Blue Book, and ask for an explanation of the sightings.

Ruppelt hadn't conducted an investigation of the sightings at that point. But he had spoken to an air force radar specialist who believed the sightings were caused by temperature inversion, a condition that can cause radar signals to bend and give false alarms. That was a safer assumption than suggesting something extraordinary. So that's what Ruppelt told Truman.

This facile conclusion assumes the kind of dogmatic worldview that Sheldrake addresses in his book. *There are no aliens here so there is nothing to investigate.* Such dogma makes abductions easy to write off, to laugh at. Just because you have inexplicable physical scars, a missing pregnancy, deep psychological trauma and memories of being abducted doesn't mean it relates to an alien abduction, no matter what you remember taking place. The message is *don't trust your thoughts and memories, don't trust your own perceptions and experiences.*

When you think about this for longer than a few seconds, you undoubtedly sense the flaws in this picture and experience an emotional resistance to the very notion. *What? My experiences don't count? They mean nothing? The encounter never happened? The abduction was a farce?*

"Materialism 'at all costs,'" wrote Sheldrake, "demands the denial of reality of our own minds and personal experiences…"

We'll look deeper at the puzzle in the final chapter.

CHAPTER 12
WHAT'S UP?

One evening in February of 2011, we stood outside Abbondanza, an Italian restaurant on Simonton Street in Key West and watched a tall, elderly man amble slowly across the street. We hadn't seen Jim Moseley in more than 20 years, but we recognized him immediately. We would soon find that at even at age 80 Jim's wit remained sharp and he still maintained a bit of his New York hipster attitude.

We had kept in touch with him since the late 1980s when we wrote for OMNI and occasionally used Moseley as a background source for UFO-related stories. He had had been writing about the subject for 60 years.

He started a UFO magazine, *Saucer New,* in 1954 and traveled the country interviewing many of the so-called 'contactees,' people who claimed close encounters with aliens. He even managed to interview ex-president Harry Truman, who had been in office during the wave of sightings over the capital in 1952. Truman denied knowing anything about UFOs.

Later, Moseley lived in Peru for several years and collected ancient artifacts. He continued his pursuit of the UFO enigma over the years and co-authored a satirical tome, *Shockingly Close to the Truth,* that combined his interests in 'grave robbing' and UFOs. From 1981 until the fall of 2012, he published a 'trade journal' for ufologists called *Saucer Smear.*

As the title suggests, Moseley used his wry sense of humor to skew both believers and skeptics who often battled each other on the pages of the journal. Jim never wrote about UFO sightings per se, only about the people investigating them. He considered himself a 'skeptical believer,' but questioned many of the major UFO cases, including the Roswell crash in 1947.

The long-time resident of Key West joined us for dinner that evening. After all these years, we wanted to know what he thought about UFOs. Right away, he told us that the 'nuts and bolts' explanation didn't ring true. In other words, UFOs are not crafts flown here from other planets in the same sense that we would fly a spacecraft to the moon or Mars. He shrugged. "Beyond that, it's all guesswork."

On abductions: "I can't say it's true because I've never experienced it. However, something is happening, what it is, who knows." His comment reminded us of lyrics from the famous Buffalo Springfield song, *For What it's Worth.*

Later, Moseley suggested that UFOs and paranormal phenomenon are related. "It's complicated. I call it the 3 ½ D explanation. It makes the most sense." When we asked what was the most important thing he had learned about UFOs over the years, he thought about a moment, then smiled. "You can't be in a hurry to find answers in a field where there aren't any." A classic Moseley comment.

After dinner, he invited us to his home. After dinner, he invited us to his home. Years earlier, we had stayed at Rose Lane Gardens, a six-unit guest house Moseley had owned in Key West's Old Town. Now, however, he lived in a dingy one-room apartment where he typed *Smear* on an old Selectric typewriter while sitting on his bed. He didn't own a computer, didn't want one. It was sad and depressing to see him living this way.

Before we departed, Moseley told us there would only be a few more issues of *Smear* before he gave it up. He mentioned health problems. It was the last time we saw him. Jim Moseley died of cancer on Nov. 16, 2012.

THE ENIGMA

In spite of the abundance of available information on UFOs, encounters, sightings, and abductions, the entire field remains an enigma, a bewildering maze. Hopefully, we'll eventually arrive at the core truth, or something close to it.

The problem is that there isn't any single core truth. Nothing is black or white.

Whether it's abductions or the crafts or the aliens themselves or what the government knows or doesn't know, there are innumerable layers and detours and distractions. What begins as a simple quest for truth about anything concerning UFOs and aliens—where they are from, what they want, how we are connected with them—leads into a strange, dark and mysterious forest where nothing is what it seems.

WHERE ARE THEY FROM?

One of the main scientific arguments against the existence of UFOs and aliens is the tremendous distances these crafts would have to travel in order to reach Earth. Yes, there might be ways to fold space, or move through wormholes, so that the journey wouldn't take quite so long. Even though there's no observable evidence of wormholes, they could exist theoretically. Still, even with a wormhole shortcut, the journey to Earth from another planet or galaxy could take a couple of human lifetimes.

In the various versions of *Star Trek,* this problem was solved by *warp drive,* where the Enterprise suddenly moves faster than the speed of light. It does this by creating an artificial skin or bubble of normal space-time that surrounds the ship. But suppose the Earth is surrounded by a kind of *membrane,* "floating in an eleven dimensional space time?" wrote Michio Kaku in *Physics of the Impossible.* "Moreover, not all these dimensions had to be small. In fact, some of these dimensions might actually be infinite."

In other words, string theory hints at the possibility of parallel universes. Is it possible, then, that UFOs are not from other planets or stars systems, but from parallel universes?

But quantum physics doesn't stop there. There's also a many worlds theory. As Michio Kaku explained in his book *Parallel Universes,* "Any universe that can exist, does. The more bizarre the universe, the less likely it is, but nonetheless these universes exist. This means there is a parallel world in which the Nazis won World War II, or a world where the Spanish Armada was never defeated and everyone is speaking in Spanish."

In Hollywood, one of the best depictions of the multiverse is *Sliding Doors,* in which a London woman's love life and career depend on whether she catches a particular train. The viewer sees the consequences of both possibilities. In terms of your own life, then, there is a version of reality where you married your current spouse and a version where you didn't. There's a version where you and your partner didn't have children or where you had many children. It isn't always either/or, but the sharply contrasting scenario helps to drive home the point that what you see is not necessarily all that exists.

So, is it possible that UFOs are from one of the multiverses where Earth suffered some terrible calamity and humanity was forced to flee? Is it possible, as other writers and researchers have speculated, that the aliens are *us?*

Whitley Strieber, in *Solving the Communion Enigma,* explored this possibility. He noted that the existence of a multiverse could explain some of the weird effects associated with contact. "Could there be some way to cross between parallel universes? But even if you could, you would not be real in any other universe you entered...perhaps what we are looking at when we look at our visitors is, in our universe, essentially not real."

He speculates that "the whole anomalous enterprise may be an apparition being projected here by some sort of arcane technology or mental state that enables a crossing of the invisible gap between the worlds. So might they not be us in another state?"

If the aliens are us from another dimension, another version of Earth that developed far differently, they are still aliens from elsewhere. The same would be the case if aliens instigated intelligent life on Earth millions of years ago.

Clearly, the UFO phenomenon seems to be connected with psychic experiences. Charles and Helene Fontaine experienced a rash of synchronicities in the aftermath of their encounter. On several occasions, Bruce Gernon predicted he would see a UFO, and then he did. Carl Jung in his book *Flying Saucers*, published in 1958, suggested that those who witness UFOs might be glimpsing images from the collective unconscious of mankind just as they might while dreaming what the Aborigines call a Big Dream—one that carries enormous significance.

Possible UFO sightings, even abductions, are both physical and psychic events. They might appear in Western culture as mysterious flying crafts, while in an isolated sea-oriented culture in earlier times, a UFO might materialize as a ghost ship, as in the case of the Caleuche (chapter one).

A PERSONAL STORY

Our own experiences support this link between the psychic and the physical. Shortly after we met in the early 1980s, we discovered a mutual interest in psychic phenomena and unexplained mysteries. Previously, we had both felt isolated in this interest, and wondered why others we knew had no interest in such topics. So one evening we decided to experiment with a Ouija board.

Yes, you read that correctly. We're aware that some people abhor the very notion of using Ouija boards, that they are sometimes associated with demonic or satanic forces or ghosts with malign intentions. We didn't attach any such idea to the board. For us, it was simply another tool for divination, similar to tarot cards, the I Ching, astrology or runes.

At first, the planchette barely moved across the board. But soon it began spelling out words. Supposedly, we were communicating—not with a spirit—but with an alien entity named Adehe, who was in a nearby spaceship. We were well aware that Ouija boards were notorious for providing information that can't be substantiated. Just ask the 'Ouija spirit' who he or she was in a past life and you might get a name, date of birth, place of residence, and other details. But none of it can be verified.

We were impressed that we actually received a coherent message, crazy as it was. We didn't take the comment seriously, but asked for proof just to see what would come through next. "If there is someone in an alien craft communicating with us through a Ouija board, then we want to see your ship."

To our surprise, we received an answer. The lights in the room blinked twice, then the planchette spelled out, "Go to airport tonight."

The blinking of the lights was a bit spooky, but okay, it could be a temporary glitch in the Florida Power and Light infrastructure. But hey, a UFO was going to appear over Fort Lauderdale International Airport? Well, if it happened, it would certainly look like proof of—well, something. We thought about it awhile, then thought, *What the hell, why not? It's only a few miles away.*

At the time, the airport was moderate in size and you could easily park along a fence on the outskirts and watch planes take off and land. We were a new couple and the plan had a romantic, wacky, adventurous feel to it. Of course, if anyone were to ask us the next day what we'd done the night before, we weren't about to say we had gone to the airport to look for a UFO. This was the early 1980s, after all.

We drove south and parked outside the airport. We remained for about an hour, until nearly 2 a.m. Nothing happened, as far as we could tell. There were no UFOs hovering overhead, no bright beams of lights shining down on us, nothing at all. We left feeling a bit foolish. *Tricked by a Ouija board*. But, well, what had we really expected?

The next morning Rob, who was working for a daily newspaper in South Florida, was assigned to cover an early school board meeting and call in a story by 10:30 a.m. He was tired from the night before, but managed to make the deadline. His editor told him to come to the office and write a longer version of the story for the second edition.

So an hour later, he was facing his second deadline of the morning. These were the days before smoking was banned in offices and the reporter at the next desk, a young woman named Susan, seemed to keep a cigarette lit constantly. On this particular morning, she was typing and puffing madly away. Rob turned in his story about the same time she finished hers and asked what she'd been working on.

"A UFO story. Broward deputies saw a UFO last night right over Perry Airport," she said with a quick laugh.

This small, local airport catered to private pilots with single or twin-engine planes. It was located in Hollywood, Florida, about ten miles from Fort Lauderdale. "You're kidding," Rob blurted.

Susan had a sarcastic streak and snapped, "It's probably from Ur-anus."

Rob's story appeared in the local section, while Susan's ran across the bottom of the front page.

That night, we drove to Perry Airport. The airport was closed, the terminal and runway lost in the dark. Like the previous night, we waited outside the fence, watching the black sky. We didn't have much time, though, and left less than an hour later, disappointed that we hadn't seen anything. It seemed Adehe was a trickster, but we'd gotten more than we'd expected.

As we drove off in separate cars, Rob turned on the radio and scrolled through the FM stations. He paused as he heard something unusual, a modern spin-off of the old dramas that once dominated radio before television. To his astonishment, this particular drama featured an alien being who had come to Earth. It was a synchronicity, and he could almost hear the trickster laughing hysterically in the background.

Believers might see this bizarre series of events as proof of alien contact, while skeptics wouldn't think twice about it. To us, it was evidence that the UFO/alien encounter phenomenon is connected with inner space as well as outer space, with non-physical reality as well as physical reality. It might even be linked with the dead and the after-life.

ALIENS AND THE AFTERLIFE

When Connie was just 17, she lost her father to brain cancer. Harry Eugene Thomas was only 42 at the time. He had been a cattleman since graduating from high school and was still a cattleman when he was diagnosed.

As he lay dying at Emory Hospital in Atlanta, he couldn't speak or see; the cancer had eaten away his speech center and destroyed his olfactory nerves. Yet, at the moment of his death, he opened his eyes and pointed at the window and said, "There's a big ship over there. I'm going to get on it."

Since it was medically impossible for him to see, much less speak, and because this impossibility was witnessed by medical personnel, his case was written up in several medical journals. Connie believes that certain groups of aliens are connected to the human afterlife, and that her father had joined them when he died.

"I know how insane that sounds. But I also know my father couldn't speak or see at that point, yet he did both. There are obviously highly-evolved entities around as well as the ones who are harmful. I am no longer taken by the Grays and their handlers, but I am nonetheless still tagged, tracked, and monitored."

If you recall from chapter 2, the high strangeness Charles Fontaine experienced in March of 2011 actually started when he and his father were in a cemetery, taking photos of family graves in order to establish a family tree. To recap: While Charles was snapping photos, his father was on the other side of the graveyard and suddenly sensed a malign presence nearby and felt a nearly overpowering urge to flee. A voice seemed to whisper in his head: Tell your son to get away from there. Get him away quickly.

Even though Charles heard his father shouting, he had trouble finding him. That evening while Charles was in his car he felt a stabbing pain in his stomach, started sweating profusely, felt a wetness in his pants and pulled into a gas station. In the restroom, he discovered that blood filled his pants.

Was the incident in the cemetery related to the dramatic UFO encounter Charles experienced nine days later in his backyard? Even if you don't know much about alien abductions, you might still know one thing—that many abductees are subjected to anal probes. Surprisingly, subsequent medical tests for Charles proved negative for colon cancer. No polyps in the colon or any sign of cancer. Did something happen in the graveyard that set him up for the encounter days later? If so, does that hint at a possible connection between aliens and the afterlife?

WHO ARE THEY, WHAT DO THEY WANT?

If we are to take the word of those who claim to have experienced close encounters, then there is no easy answer to these questions.

Diane has encountered beings that span the spectrum of possibilities— "angelic, demonic, and everything else in between." Connie believes there are at least three groups of ETs interacting with humans. "One group is ominous and their agenda is to annihilate our species. A second group is neutral, with its own agenda. This group doesn't have any particular intent to harm us, but if we are harmed in their pursuit of their agenda, well, too bad. The third group is highly evolved and has the best interests of our species as its agenda, an agenda of protection."

Yet, the Grays seem to be the predominant entities that have seeped into our awareness, and the stories of encounters seem to point to genetic experiments aimed at creating a hybrid race. If that's the case, are there hybrids among us? What are they and their creators planning for the planet? Will they save us or destroy us?

If there are benevolent aliens, abductees who have only experienced the worst of them might wonder where they are. Here's a personal story that seems to suggest contact with more benevolent beings.

THE 3 CURIOUS ALIENS

In October 2001, a month after 9-11, Trish and writer Nancy Pickard traveled to Alabama to attend a workshop taught by Eric Pearl, an L.A. chiropractor and the author of The Reconnection.

For 12 years, Pearl ran a successful chiropractic practice. Then his patients began reporting that they felt his hands on them — even though he wasn't physically touching them. Patients soon reported miraculous healings from cancers, AIDS-related diseases, epilepsy, chronic fatigue syndrome, rheumatoid arthritis and osteoarthritis, birth disfigurements, cerebral palsy and other serious afflictions. All this occurred when Pearl simply held his hands near them. He realized he had tapped into something and began exploring this energy.

The book is compelling and Trish and Nancy decided it was worth the fee and the airfare to attend the two-day workshop and find out what Pearl was about. The workshop was conducted in a massive meeting room at one of the large hotels in Birmingham. There were at least two hundred people in attendance. After Pearl introduced his material, he demonstrated a particular hand movement that all attendees were to practice on a stranger. "Team up," he said. "And let's give this a try."

So people paired up. Trish's partner, about whom she recalls nothing, went first.

There were massage tables set up in the room and Trish stretched out on one while her partner stood beside it. Lying on her back, she shut her eyes and her partner began to sweep her hands over and around Trish's body, but without touching it. Trish realized the woman's hands were moving through her energy field, and that she could *feel* the sweeping motions.

Suddenly, Trish's hair stood on end. She felt as though she'd stuck her finger in an electrical socket and that she was being shocked beyond comprehension. It wasn't painful, just abrupt and astonishing. A moment later, a column of light shot out of her forehead and penetrated the ceiling. Even though her eyes were closed, she could *see* this column of light.

At the very top of it, she saw three beings crowded around, sort of jostling each other like kids eager for a better view. They watched her, watched everyone in the room, intensely curious about what was going on. Trish never felt threatened by them.

Later, when Pearl asked people in the group what they had experienced, Trish mentioned the sensation that her hair was being pulled, the column of light, and the three entities that seemed to be observing the workshop. Pearl acknowledged that he felt there was an inter-dimensional component to his work.

Skip ahead three years. In June 2004, Hurricane Frances hit our area. It was a large, sloppy storm that, at one point, covered most of the Florida peninsula. It stalled for fifteen hours and dumped more than a foot of rain over South Florida. Early on, water began seeping under our front door. During the long hours that Frances pounded away at our neighborhood, we worried about our skylights leaking. Everyone in a hurricane area knows that if your roof is compromised in a hurricane, your house is pretty much history.

We were bunked in the bedroom with our daughter, a dog, three cats, and a bird. About five that morning, Trish was the only one still awake. The rain pounded relentlessly at the hurricane shutters. She heard the skylights vibrating in the living room, the kitchen, the bathroom. She considered getting up to check the skylights and front door, but was so exhausted she lay there for another moment. And suddenly, a beam of light shot out of her forehead, pierced the bedroom ceiling, and she saw those three entities at the top of the column, peering down at her.

Right then, she knew the house would come through the storm intact, that there wasn't any danger, and immediately fell asleep. When she woke a few hours later, the storm had moved on and the house was fine.

What's really interesting about this is that Trish didn't recall that these three entities looked like aliens until she was talking to Anne and Whitley Strieber about synchronicity on one of their Dreamland radio show some years later.

So what were these three curious little beings? Good-guy aliens? Interdimensional beings? Her imagination?

SEEKING CONSENSUS

One of the primary challenges in researching and writing about this material is that it doesn't fit into consensus reality—the physical world as we know it right now. Yet, our consensus reality constantly evolves.

When Columbus set out from Spain for the New World, the consensus reality was that the earth was flat. Galileo was imprisoned by the Catholic Church because he defied the consensus reality that insisted the Earth was at the center of the universe and the sun revolved around it. Instead, Galileo proclaimed that the Earth and other planets revolved around the sun.

Until 1865 in the U.S., it was *legal* to *own* another human being. The thirteenth amendment to the constitution ended that. Until the passage of the nineteenth amendment in 1920, women weren't allowed to vote. In both instances, consensus reality lay in a belief that blacks and women were somehow inferior to white men.

You get the idea. Throughout time, certain consensus beliefs have imprisoned us, kept us from evolving as a species, as individuals.

When the consensus reality becomes so stifling, it's like a cancer that eats away at the collective human spirit. Discontent collapses into anger, then rage, rebellion ensues, and the consensus changes and evolves. That's how new paradigms are born. This is what happened during the Sixties with the Civil Rights movement and Vietnam War protests. It happened in 1989, when the Berlin Wall fell. In the aftermath of the financial meltdown in 2008, it has happened with the Occupy Movement, the Arab Spring, and Surround the Congress, a global resistance movement against Europe's economic austerity measures.

At these various junctures throughout history, the masses have risen up and their collective energy has clashed with the Powers That Be—churches, inquisitors, governments, Wall Street, banks, corporations, dictators, the military, oppressors, the people in charge. Even when the uprisings don't seem to work—like the faceoff in China's Tiananmen Square—consensus reality is still altered in some ways.

We are witnessing what Hindus called Indra's Net, a great spiritual net in which everyone and everything in the cosmos is connected. *What affects you, affects me.* In quantum physics, this underlying hidden reality, or universal consciousness, is known as the non-local mind.

"Operating outside the boundaries of normal space and time, it is the great organizing and unifying force in the universe, infinite in scope and duration," wrote Deepak Chopra in *The Spontaneous Fulfillment of Desire.* "By its nature, nonlocal mind connects all things because it *is* all things."

The famous Swiss psychologist Carl Jung called it the collective unconscious and the French philosopher and Jesuit priest Pierre Teilhard de Chardin called it the noosphere, an invisible web linking all existence. He proposed that as mankind organizes itself in more complex social networks, the noosphere expands in awareness.

As this non-local mind, this "great organizing and unifying force" grows and swells, a change in consensus reality becomes inevitable. It may not happen quickly or peacefully, but one way or another, it happens. And perhaps the consensus reality regarding UFOs and aliens has nearly reached this point of collapse.

In the days before Google, the Internet, smart phones, iPads, in the days when you got your news mainly through newspapers, TV network news or radio, in the days before the world was connected through social media, UFO sightings were rarely reported. And when they were it was often in a light-hearted, joking manner. *Nothing here, nothing to be taken seriously.*

But in this second decade of the twenty-first century, news and information are practically instantaneous. There are witnesses to *everything*. A tweet that travels around the world in a matter of seconds can turn a small demonstration into a mass movement. A You Tube video can go viral and galvanize millions.

As a species, we are now so interconnected technologically that with the tap of a few keys, we can find out where in the world the latest UFO sightings and encounters have occurred. The UFO community is so well organized now that MUFON—the Mutual UFO Network—has chapters in every state and more than 30 foreign countries, provides live maps on its website of sightings, with photos and videos when available, and the latest updates on encounters and sightings. Whitley Strieber's site, unknowncountry.com, has a page where you can report sightings, encounters, and abductions. Websites abound.

We're connected. And yet, the mystery and paradox about UFOs, aliens, and abductions remains and science is partially to blame. The concept of alien life visiting Earth isn't part of the current scientific paradigm.

WHAT DOES IT MEAN?

"If we don't find something positive and life-affirming in the frequent horror of these experiences," Connie Cannon says, "then we can't survive them intact. In our overt consciousness, these experiences don't make sense.

There's no compartment in our human species where these experiences can be placed."

There's no doubt in Connie's mind that she has had encounters with the worst of the worst of these entities, and with the best. "I hold on tightly to those experiences that are the best of the best. Without these, I would have long ago been put in permanent lockdown. I have released my fears and somehow understand that somewhere within each of us, the answers lay buried."

So maybe we *do* have a space for these experiences. We just need to know how to dig deeply enough to find that space. We need to ask the right questions. With this recognition can come a kind of peace with the encounters. As Connie says: "What can they do, but destroy my body and attempt to destroy my mind and control me? They can't destroy my soul. They can't destroy my essence. Knowing this, I no longer fear them."

For Charles Fontaine, the life-changing encounter in his backyard has rocked his reality. The solid foundations of his life have shifted. He now accepts the reality of what not so long ago he considered to be fictional or just the bizarre thoughts of crazy people. A year and a half after his encounter, he confided that not a day had gone by without a thought about 'them'—the ones behind his encounter.

"I constantly try to understand just why they sent me signs—these synchronicities—day after day for more than six months after the encounter. Then suddenly it stopped."

Possibly, during the first months, Charles was experiencing a dual reality. He was still clinging to his old way of thinking, his comfortable belief system, but was also puzzling daily about a new awareness that was evolving as a result of his encounter. His mind was torn in two directions and during this confusing time when he was uncertain about what was real, he experienced startling and meaningful coincidences that seemed to guide him along a new path.

Perhaps the synchronicities were generated by his own consciousness during that time frame, and they stopped when his mind shifted to a new way of thinking, a willingness to accept a new personal reality. Maybe that was what the experience was all about for him. He took an interest in something unusual in his backyard, and stumbled into a new reality, like Alice tumbling down the rabbit hole.

• • •

By the end of 2012, Charles had made peace with himself and with his experience. "Time has brought me back on track. Do not get me wrong here, the experience is still with me, but now with a touch of Zen. I accept the fact that they exist and that I have no choice but to live with this new reality, even though others do not believe it. But I no longer feel that urge to scream out to people on the street and tell them that they exist. They will find out for themselves."

ABOUT THE AUTHORS

ROB & TRISH MACGREGOR reside in South Florida. They write fiction and non-fiction. Both have won the Mystery Writers of America Edgar Allan Poe Award. Trish's latest novel is *Ghost Key*. Rob's latest novel is *Time Catcher*. Their most recent non-fiction books are *The 7 Secrets of Synchronicity* and *Synchronicity and the Other Side*. They also co-authored *The Everything Dream Book* and *The Lotus & the Stars: The Way of Astro-Yoga*. Trish is also the author of *Power Tarot* and Rob is the author of *Psychic Power* and co-author of *The Fog* (with Bruce Gernon).

Curious about other Crossroad Press books?
Stop by our site:
https://www.crossroadpress.com
We offer quality writing
in digital, audio, and print formats.

www.ingramcontent.com/pod-product-compliance
Lightning Source LLC
Chambersburg PA
CBHW020127180626
46810CB00004B/1434